THE WHITE CAT

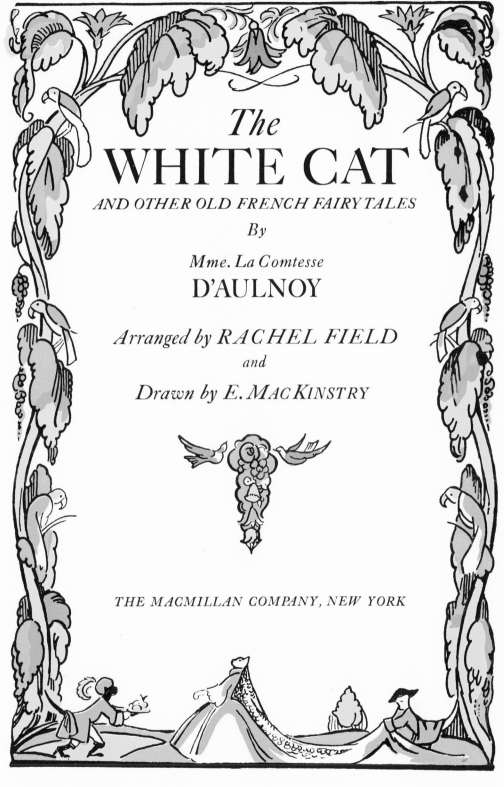

The WHITE CAT

AND OTHER OLD FRENCH FAIRY TALES

By

Mme. La Comtesse
D'AULNOY

Arranged by RACHEL FIELD
and

Drawn by E. MACKINSTRY

THE MACMILLAN COMPANY, NEW YORK

To
Mme. la Comptesse d'Esgrigny,
this book.

CONTENTS

INTRODUCTION

DEAR CHILDREN:

MARIE CATHERINE LE JUMELLE DE BERNE-VILLE, *afterwards Mme. La Comptesse D'Aulnoy* * *who wrote these tales, was I fear something of an adventuress. So are we all of us, every man, woman and child on this globe, adventurers. What I mean is that not all of her adventures were admirable.*

It was in the time of Louis XIV, and, like full bottom wigs, Romance was the fashion. Little Marie Catherine was born in 1655, and her mother, she hints, was too young and too pretty a woman of fashion to enjoy a growing, let alone a grown up daughter. Marie Catherine was sent to a convent school and at the ages of twelve to fifteen began her career of letters. Very literally so, for she copied out long-winded love letters from Romances and Novels of the period and sent them to one of her professors, M. de Blossac. The good man enjoyed them hugely until the nuns got wind of it, and then there was outcry and scandal. The small penitent, with mamma behind her, was all for becoming a nun, but M. le Jumelle de Berneville, who seems to have been a man of humor and sense, eloped with his own daughter in a coach and four. And in this coach was waiting, just like a Fairy Tale, a charming young husband, François de la Mothe, Sieur d'Aulnoy.

Later the mother and daughter seem to have combined together against the Compte d'Aulnoy, and there is a hint of his having been charged with lèse-majesté (or treason against the king), but escaping it triumphantly. And there is another rumor of Mme. d'Aulnoy having known far too intimately a certain notorious Madame Tiquet, beheaded for the murder of her husband. Later still Marie Catherine and her mother turned up at the court of Charles the Second, plunged into its intrigue and tittle tattle, and she wrote a Memoir of the Court of England, full of assumed names and dubious episodes, rather like a poor play.

In short Mme. d'Aulnoy seems forever to have moved in high society

* D'Aulnoy = Dóle-nwa.

INTRODUCTION

and about courts, but forever on the under, and slightly shady side. She saw the glass coaches, the palaces as dazzling as those of Fairyland, the silks and satins, the powdered wigs, the queens and princes, almost as powerful to bestow wealth and happiness as a Beneficent Fairy or an Enchanted Prince, but like her own adorable White Cat, she saw them from under a veil. "I am generally so unfortunate in matters that concern me," says the little White Cat. Yes, there was a head and tail to be cut away before the beautiful Princess could appear.

That there was something wistfully away from all this intrigue and back stair gossip, we may surmise, for always, and through all Mme. d'Aulnoy wrote her Fairy Tales. Always through the stilted sentiment, and the Court Life which she so evidently loved, is the idea of disguise, misfortune, and a rescue. Perhaps the White Cat is a Romance with a Key.

Time seems to have cut away the disguise, not swiftly but gently. We have a final glimpse of Mme. d'Aulnoy keeping a School for Young Ladies in England, and with two wise and witty daughters of her own. Of one of them, Mme. de Héere,* wife of the President de Vertron, a contemporary writes:

> In the prose and the verse of pleasing Héere,
> I speak as I think it, ma foi!
> A likeness to Madame her mother is there;
> All the wit and the charm of d'Aulnoy.

"All the wit and the charm of d'Aulnoy!" . . . and how children love her Fairy Tales, told and retold, in all collections, and in every language!

It is a good thing when our own creations turn out well in the end.

And so we leave her, an old lady in an English park, perhaps telling the adventures of the White Cat to a little boy and girl who listen entranced in the green shadow, wondering if her ebony cane is possibly a wand. Through the emerald tunnel of the leaves she seems to smile, head on one side, . . . indulgent, a trifle surprised that of all her adventures those in Fairyland alone remain.

THE TEXT used here is that of Monsieur Planché, a Frenchman who translated the Tales literally, in the early sixties of the last century.

They are arranged and abridged by Miss Rachel Field, herself a poet and a delightful writer of Children's Stories.

* Héere = Hay-áir

INTRODUCTION

The Artist *spent a year in France, steeping herself again in the long loved traditions of the Seventeenth and Eighteenth Centuries, and thanks the Editor, Miss Louise Seaman, for making this book possible.*

But the real illustrator of the book was a little American girl who lived with her mother in Paris.

She loved the pictures of the people of the times of these Fairy Tales, their pale silks and satins, curly wigs, old parks and old chateaux. She loved the Tales, first told her by an old French nurse.

She dreamed the people, and the cats, and the book in blue and pink, just as you see it. And you can see her dreaming about it on the last page of all, with long golden hair.

I will tell you a secret. Her hair was rough, and dark, and cropped, but she wanted to have long, flowing golden locks, and that is why she has them in the picture.

. . . As Mme. d'Aulnoy would understand.

ELIZABETH MacKINSTRY.

THE WHITE CAT

THE WHITE CAT

ONCE upon a time there was a King who had three sons. The day came when they were grown so big and strong that he began to fear they would be planning to rule in his place. This would cause trouble among themselves and his subjects. Now the King was not so young as he once had been but nevertheless he had no notion of giving up his kingdom then and there. So after much thought he hit upon a scheme which should keep them too busily occupied to interfere in the affairs of state. Accordingly he called the three into his private apartments where he spoke to them with great kindliness and concern of his plans for their future.

"I am planning to retire from the affairs of state. But I do not wish my subjects to suffer from this change. Therefore, while I am still alive, I shall transfer my crown to one of you. I shall not follow the usual custom of leaving the crown to my eldest son, but whichever one of you shall bring me the handsomest and most intelligent little dog shall become my heir."

The Princes were greatly surprised by this strange request, but they could not very well refuse to humor their father's whim; and since there was luck in it for the two younger sons and the elder of the three was a timid, rather spiritless fellow, they agreed readily enough. The King then bade

them farewell after first distributing jewels and money among them and adding that a year from that day at the same place and hour they should return to him with their little dogs.

Within sight of the city gates stood a castle where the three often spent many days in company with their young companions. Here they agreed to part and to meet again in a year before proceeding with their trophies to the King; and so having pledged their good faith, and changing their names that they might not be known, each set off upon a different road.

It would take far too long to recount the adventures of all three Princes so I shall tell only of those that befell the youngest, for a more gay and

well-mannered Prince never lived, nor one so handsome and accomplished.

Scarcely a day passed that he did not buy a dog or two, greyhounds, mastiffs, bloodhounds, pointers, spaniels, water dogs, lapdogs; but the instant he found a handsomer one he let the first go and kept the new purchase, since it would have been impossible for him to carry them all on his journeyings. He went without fixed plan or purpose and so he continued for many days until at last darkness and a terrible storm overtook him at nightfall in a lonely forest. Thunder and lightning rumbled and flashed; rain fell in torrents; the trees seemed to close more densely about him until at last he could no longer find his way. When he had wandered thus for some time he suddenly saw a glint of light between the tree trunks. Feeling certain that this must mean a shelter of some sort he pressed on till he found himself approaching the most magnificent castle he had ever seen. The gate was of gold and covered with jewels of such brilliance that it was their light which had guided him to the spot. In spite of the rain and storm he caught glimpses of walls of finest porcelain decorated with pictures of the most famous fairies from the beginning of the world up to that very day: Cinderella, Graciosa, Sleeping Beauty, and a hundred others. As he admired all this magnificence he noticed a rabbit's foot fastened to the golden gates

THE WHITE CAT

by a chain of diamonds. Marveling greatly at such
a lavish display of precious gems, the young Prince
pulled at the rabbit's foot and straightway an unseen bell of wonderful sweetness rang; the gate
was opened by hundreds of tiny hands and others
pushed him forward while he hesitated amazed
upon the threshold. He moved on wonderingly, his
hand on the hilt of his sword until he was reassured
by two voices singing a welcome. Again he felt
himself being pushed, this time toward a gate of
coral opening upon an apartment of mother-of-
pearl from which he passed into others still more
richly decorated and alight with wax candles and
great chandeliers sparkling with a thousand rain-
bows.

5

He had passed through perhaps sixty such rooms when the hands that guided him made a sign for him to stop. He saw a large armchair moving by itself toward a fireplace at the same moment that the fire began to blaze and the hands, which he now observed to be very small and white, carefully drew off his wet clothes and handed him others so fine and richly embroidered they seemed fit for a wedding day. The hands continued to dress him, until at last, powdered and attired more handsomely than he had ever been in his life before, the Prince was led into a banquet hall. Here the four walls were decorated solely with paintings representing famous cats, Puss-in-Boots and others whom he was quick to recognize. Even more astonishing than this was the table set for two with its gold service and crystal cups.

There was an orchestra composed entirely of cats. One held a music book with the strangest notes imaginable; another beat time with a little baton; and all the rest strummed tiny guitars.

While the Prince stared in amazement, each cat suddenly began to mew in a different key and to claw at the guitar strings. It was the strangest music ever heard! The Prince would have thought himself in bedlam had not the palace itself been so marvelously beautiful. So he stopped his ears and laughed heartily at the various poses and grimaces of these strange musicians. He was meditating upon the extraordinary sights he had already seen in the castle, when he beheld a little figure entering the hall. It was scarcely more than two feet in height and wrapped in a long gold crêpe veil. Before it walked two cats dressed in deep mourning and wearing cloaks and swords, while still others followed, some carrying rat-traps full of rats and mice in cages.

By this time the Prince was too astonished to think. But presently the tiny pink figure approached him and lifted its veil. He now beheld the most beautiful little white cat that ever was or ever will be. She had such a very youthful and melancholy air and a mewing so soft and sweet that it went straight to the young Prince's heart.

"Son of a King," she said to him, "thou art welcome; my mewing Majesty beholds thee with pleasure."

"Madam," responded the Prince, bowing as low as possible before her, "it is very gracious of you to receive me with so much attention, but you do not appear to me to be an ordinary little cat. The gift of speech which you have and this superb castle you inhabit are certainly evidence to the contrary."

"Son of a King," rejoined the White Cat, "I pray that you will cease to pay me compliments. I am plain in my speech and manners, but I have a kind heart. Come," she added, to her attendants, "let them serve supper and bid the concert cease, for the Prince does not understand what they are singing."

"And are they singing words, madam?" he asked incredulously.

"Certainly," she answered, "we have very gifted poets here, as you will see if you remain long enough."

Supper was then served to them by the same hands that had guided him there, and a very strange meal it was. There were two dishes of each course —one soup, for instance, being of savory pigeons while the other had been made of nicely fattened mice. The sight of this rather took away the Prince's appetite until his hostess, who seemed to guess what was passing in his mind, assured him that his own dishes had been specially prepared and contained no rats and mice of any kind. Her charming manners convinced the Prince that the little Cat had no wish to deceive him, so he began to eat and drink with great enjoyment. During their meal he happened to observe that on one paw she wore a tiny miniature set in a bracelet. This surprised him so that he begged her to let him examine it more closely. He had supposed it would be the picture of Master Puss, but what was his astonishment to find it the portrait of a handsome young man who bore a strange resemblance to himself! As he stared at it, the White Cat was heard to sigh so deeply and with such profound

8

sadness that the Prince became even more curious; but he dared not question one so affected. Instead he entertained her with tales of court life, with which, to his surprise, he found her well acquainted.

After supper the White Cat led her guest into another Hall, where upon a little stage twelve cats and twelve monkeys danced in the most fantastic costumes. So the evening ended in great merriment; and after the Cat had bade the Prince a gracious good night the same strange hands conducted him to his own apartment, where in spite of the softness of his bed he spent half the night trying to solve the mystery of the castle and his extraordinary little hostess.

But when morning came he was no nearer to

an answer to his questionings, so he allowed the pair of hands to help him dress and lead him into the palace courtyard. Here a vast company of cats in hunting costume were gathering to the sound of the horn. A fête day indeed! The White Cat was going to hunt and wished the Prince to accompany her. Now the mysterious hands presented him with a wooden horse. He made some objection to mounting it, but it proved to be an excellent charger, and a tireless galloper. The White Cat rode beside him on a monkey, the handsomest and proudest that ever was seen. She had thrown off her long veil and wore a military cap which made her look so bold that she frightened all the mice in the neighborhood. Never was there a more successful hunt. The cats outran all the rabbits and hares and a thousand skillful feats were performed to the gratification of the entire company. Tiring of the hunt at last the White Cat took up a horn no bigger than the Prince's little finger and blew upon it with so loud and clear a tone it could be heard ten leagues away. Scarcely had she sounded two or three flourishes when all the cats in the countryside seemed to appear. By land and sea and through the air they all came flocking to her call, dressed in every conceivable costume. So, followed by this extraordinary train, the Prince rode back with his hostess to the castle.

That night the White Cat put on her gold veil

again and they dined together as before. Being very hungry the Prince ate and drank heartily, and this time the food had a strange effect upon him. All recollection of his father and the little dog he was to find for him slipped from his mind. He no longer thought of anything but of gossiping with the White Cat and enjoying her kind and gracious companionship. So the days passed in pleasant sport and amusement and the nights in feasting and conversation. There was scarcely one in which he did not discover some new charm of the little White Cat. Now he had forgotten even the land of his birth. The hands continued to wait upon him and supply every want till he began to regret that he could not become a cat himself to live forever in such pleasant company.

"Alas," he confessed to the White Cat at last, "how wretched it makes me even to think of leaving you! I have come to love you so dearly. Could you not become a woman or else make me a cat?"

But though she smiled at his wish, the look she turned upon him was very strange.

A year passes away quickly when one has neither pain nor care, when one is merry and in good health. The Prince took no thought of time, but the White Cat was not so forgetful.

"There are only three days left to look for the little dog you were to bring to the King, your father," she reminded him. "Your two brothers have already found several very beautiful ones."

At her words the Prince's memory returned to him and he marveled at his strange forgetfulness.

"What spell would have made me forget what was most important to me in the whole world?" he cried in despair. "My honor and my fortune are lost unless I can find a dog that will win a kingdom for me and a horse swift enough to carry me home again in this short time!"

So, believing this to be impossible, he grew very sorrowful. Then the White Cat spoke to him with great reassurance.

"Son of a King," she said, "do not distress yourself so. I am your friend. Remain here another day, and though it is five hundred leagues from here to your country the good wooden horse will carry you there in less than twelve hours' time."

"But it is not enough for me to return to my father, dear Cat," said the Prince. "I must take him a little dog as well."

"And so you shall," replied she. "Here is a walnut which contains one more beautiful than the Dog Star."

"Your Majesty jests with me," he protested.

"Put the walnut to your ear then," insisted the Cat, "and you will hear it bark."

He obeyed her, and as he held the walnut to his ear a faint "Bow-wow" came from within, more tiny and shrill than a cricket on a winter night. The

Prince could scarcely believe his ears or contain his curiosity to see so diminutive a creature. But he was wise enough to follow the White Cat's advice not to open the walnut till he should reach his father's presence.

It was a sad leave-taking between the Prince and the White Cat. A thousand times he thanked her, but though he urged her to return to court with him, she only shook her head and sighed deeply as upon the night of his arrival. So he galloped away at last on the wooden horse, which bore him more swiftly than the wind to the appointed place.

He reached the castle even before his two brothers and enjoyed the sight of their surprise at seeing a wooden horse champing at the bit in the courtyard. The two brothers were so busy telling of their various adventures that they took little note of their younger brother's silence concerning his, but when the time came to show one another their dogs the two were vastly amused at sight of an ugly cur which the young Prince had brought along, pretending to consider it a marvel of beauty. Needless to say the elder Princes smiled with secret satisfaction to think how far superior were their own dogs, for though they wished their brother no ill luck, they had no wish to see him ruling over the kingdom.

Next morning the three set out together in the same coach. The two eldest brothers carried bas-

13

kets filled with little dogs too delicate and beautiful to be touched, while the youngest carried the poor cur as if it also was precious. By no outward sign did he betray the presence of the walnut with its precious occupant which was safely hidden in his pocket. No sooner did the three set foot in the palace than all the court crowded around to welcome the returned travelers and see the results of their journeyings. The King received them with great joy, professing delight over the little dogs his two elder sons brought out for his inspection. But the more he studied their merits, the more puzzled he became, so nearly were they alike in beauty and grace. The two brothers were already beginning to dispute with one another as to which deserved

THE WHITE CAT

the crown when the younger Brother stepped forward, holding upon the palm of his hand the walnut so lately presented to him by the White Cat. Opening it without more ado, he revealed a tiny dog lying upon cotton. So perfectly formed was it and so small that it could pass through a little finger ring without touching any part of it. It was more delicate than thistledown and its coat shone with colors of the rainbow. Nor was this all; immediately it was released from its kennel, the little creature arose on its hind legs and began to go through the steps of a tarantella, with tiny castanets and all the airs and graces of a Spanish dancer!

The King was dumbfounded and even the two brothers were forced to acknowledge that such a beautiful and gifted little dog had never been seen before. But their father was in no mood to give up his kingdom, so he announced that he had decided upon another test of their skill. This time he would give them a year to travel over land and sea in

15

search of a piece of cloth so fine it would pass through the eye of the finest Venetian-point lace needle.

So the Prince remounted his wooden horse and set off at full speed, for now he knew exactly where he wanted to go. So great was his eagerness to see the beautiful White Cat once more that he could scarcely contain himself until her castle came into view. This time every window was alight to welcome him and the faithful pair of hands which had waited on him so well before were ready to take the bridle of the wooden horse and lead it back to the stable while the Prince hurried to the White Cat's private apartments.

He found her lying on a little couch of blue satin with many pillows. Her expression was sad until she caught sight of him. Then she sprang up and began to caper about him delightedly.

"Oh, dear Prince," cried she, "I had scarcely dared to hope for your return. I am generally so unfortunate in matters that concern me."

A thousand times must the grateful Prince caress her and recount his adventures, which perhaps she knew more about than he guessed. And now he told her of his father's latest whim—how he had set his heart upon having a piece of cloth that could pass through the eye of the finest needle. For his own part he did not believe it was possible to find such a thing, but he believed that if any one could

16

help him in this quest it would be his dear White Cat. She listened attentively to all he told her and finally explained with a thoughtful air that this was a matter demanding careful consideration. There were, it seemed, some cats in her castle who could spin with extraordinary skill, and she added that she would also put a paw to the work herself so that he need not trouble himself to search farther.

The Prince was only too delighted to accept this offer and he and his charming hostess sat down to supper together, after which a magnificent display of fireworks was set off in his honor. And once more the days passed in enchanted succession. The ingenious White Cat knew a thousand different ways of entertaining her guest, so that he never once thought of missing human society. Indeed, he was probably the first person in the world to spend a whole year of complete contentment with only cats for company.

The second year slipped away as pleasantly as the first. The Prince could scarcely think of anything that the tireless hands did not instantly supply, whether books, jewels, pictures, old things or new. In short, he had but to say, "I want a certain gem that is in the cabinet of the Great Mogul, or the King of Persia, or such and such a statue in Corinth or any part of Greece," and he saw it instantly before him, without knowing how it came or who brought it. It is not unpleasant at all to find oneself able to possess any treasure in the world. No wonder our Prince was happy!

But the White Cat who was ever watchful of his welfare, warned him that the hour of departure was approaching and that he might make himself easy in his mind about the piece of cloth, for she had a most wonderful one for him. She added that it was her intention this time to furnish him with an equipage worthy of his high birth, and without waiting for his reply, beckoned him to the window overlooking the castle courtyard. Here he saw an open coach of gold and flame-color with a thousand gallant devices to please the mind and eye. It was drawn by twelve horses as white as snow, four-and-four abreast, with harnesses of flaming velvet embroidered with diamonds and gold. A hundred other coaches, each with eight horses and filled with superbly attired noblemen followed, escorted by a thousand bodyguards whose uniforms were so richly embroidered you could not see the material beneath. But the most remarkable part of this cavalcade was that a portrait of the White Cat was to be seen everywhere, in coach device, uniform, or worn as a decoration on the doublets of those who rode in the train, as if it were some newly created order that had been conferred upon them.

"Go now," said the White Cat to the Prince. "Appear at the court of the King, your father, in such magnificence that he cannot fail to be im-

The White Cat

pressed and to bestow upon you the crown which you deserve. Here is another walnut. Crack it in his presence and you will find the piece of cloth you asked of me."

"Oh, dear White Cat," he answered tenderly, "I am so overcome by your goodness that I would gladly give up my hopes of power and future grandeur to stay here with you the rest of life."

"Son of a King," she answered, "I am convinced of your kindness of heart. A kind heart is a rare thing among princes who would be loved by all, yet not love any one themselves. But you are the proof that there is an exception to this rule. I give you credit for the affection you have shown to a little white cat that after all is good for nothing but to catch mice."

So the Prince kissed her paw and departed.

This time the two brothers arrived at their father's palace before him, congratulating themselves that their young brother must be dead or gone for good. They lost no time in displaying the cloths they had brought, which were indeed so fine that they could pass through the eye of a large needle but not through the small eye of the needle the King had already selected. At this there arose a great murmuring at court. The friends of the two Princes took sides among themselves as to which had fulfilled the bargain better. But this was interrupted by a flourish of trumpets announcing the arrival of their younger brother.

The magnificence of his train fairly took away the breath of the King and his court, but their astonishment grew even greater when, after saluting his father, the young Prince brought out the walnut. This he cracked with great ceremony only to find, instead of the promised piece of cloth, a cherry stone. At sight of this the King and the court exchanged sly smiles. Nothing daunted, the Prince cracked the cherry stone, only to find a kernel inside. Jeers and murmurs ran through the great apartment. The Prince must be a fool indeed! He made no answer to them, but even he began to doubt the White Cat's words as he found next a grain of wheat and within that the smallest millet

seed. "Oh, White Cat, White Cat! Have you betrayed me?" he muttered between his teeth. Even as he spoke he felt a little scratch upon his hand,

22

so sharp that it drew blood. Taking this to be some sort of sign, the Prince proceeded to open the millet seed. Before the incredulous eyes of the whole court he drew out of it a piece of cloth four hundred yards long and marvelously embroidered with colored birds and beasts, with trees and fruits and flowers, with shells and jewels and even with suns and moons and countless stars. There were also portraits of Kings and Queens of the past upon it and of their children and children's children, not forgetting the smallest child, and each dressed perfectly in the habit of his century.

The sight of this was almost too much for the King. He could scarcely find the needle. Through its eye the wonderful piece of cloth was able to pass not only once but six times, before the jealous gaze of the two older Princes. But the King was still far from ready to give up his kingdom. Once more he turned to his children.

"I am going to put your obedience to a new and final test," he told them. "Go and travel for another year and whichever one of you brings back with him the most beautiful Princess shall marry her and be crowned King on his wedding day. I pledge my honor that after this I shall ask no further favors of you."

So off the three went again, the youngest Prince still in a good humor although he had the least cause to be since he had twice been the acknowl-

edged winner of the wager. But he was not one to
dispute his father's will, so soon he and all his train
were taking the road back to his dear White Cat.
She knew the very day and hour of his arrival, and
all along the way flowers had been strewn and perfume made the air sweet. Once more the castle gate
was opened to him and the strange hands took him
in charge while all the cats climbed into the trees
to welcome their returning visitor.

"So, my Prince," said the White Cat when he
reached her side at last, "once more you have returned without the crown. But no matter," she
added as he opened his lips to explain, "I know
that you are bound to take back the most beautiful
Princess to court and I will find one for you, never
fear. Meantime, let us amuse ourselves and be
merry."

The third year passed for the young Prince as
had the two others, and since nothing runs away
faster than time passed without trouble or care, it
is certain that he would have completely forgotten
the day of his return to court had not the White
Cat reminded him of it. This time, however, she
told him that upon him alone depended his fate.
He must promise to do whatever she asked of him.
The Prince agreed readily enough until he heard
her command him to cut off her head and tail and
fling them into the fire.

"I!" cried the Prince, aghast, "I be so barbarous

24

as to kill my dear White Cat? This is some trick to try my heart, but you should be sure of its gratitude."

"No, no, Son of a King," she answered, "I know your heart too well for that. But fate is stronger than either of us, and you must do as I bid you. It is the only way; and you must believe me, for I swear it on the honor of a Cat."

Tears came into the eyes of the Prince at the mere thought of cutting off the head of so amiable and pretty a creature. He tried to say all the most tender things he could think of, hoping to distract her. But she persisted that she wished to die by his hand because it was the only means of preventing his brothers from winning the crown. So piteously

25

did she beg him that at last, all of a tremble, he drew his sword. With faltering hand he cut off the head and tail of his dear White Cat.

Next moment the most remarkable transformation took place before his very eyes. The body of the little White Cat suddenly changed into that of a young girl, the most graceful ever seen. But this was as nothing compared to the beauty and sweetness of her face, where only the shining brightness of the eyes gave any hint of the cat she had so recently been. The Prince was struck dumb with surprise and delight. He opened his eyes wider still to look at her, and what was his amazement to behold a troop of lords and ladies entering the apartment, each with a cat's skin flung over an arm. They advanced and, throwing themselves at the feet of their Queen, expressed their joy at seeing

26

her once more restored to her natural form. She received them with great affection, but presently she desired them to leave her alone with the Prince.

"Behold, my dear Prince," she said as soon as they had done so, "I am released of a terrible enchantment, too long a tale to tell you now. Suffice it to say that this portrait which you saw upon my paw when I was a cat, was given to me by my guardian fairies during the time of my trial. I supposed it was of my first, unhappy love who was so cruelly taken from me and whose resemblance to you was so striking. Conceive my joy then, to find that it is of the Prince who has my entire heart and who was destined to rescue me from my enchantment."

And she bowed low before our Prince, who was so filled with joy and wonder that he would have

27

remained there forever telling her of his love, had
she not reminded him that the hour for his return
to his father's court was almost upon them. Taking
him by the hands, she led him into the courtyard
to a chariot even more magnificent than the one
she had provided before. The rest were equally
gorgeous, the horses shod with emeralds held in
place by diamond nails, with such gold and jeweled
trappings as were never seen before or since. But
the young Prince had eyes for nothing beyond the
beauty of his companion.

Just before they reached the outskirts of the
city, they sighted the Prince's two brothers with
their trains driving toward them from opposite
directions. At this the Princess hid herself in a
small throne of rock crystal and precious gems,
while the Prince remained alone in the coach. His
two brothers, each accompanied by a charming
lady, greeted him warmly but expressed surprise
and curiosity that he should be alone. To these
questions he replied that he had been so unfortunate as not to have met with any lady of sufficient
beauty to bring with him to court. He added, however, that he had instead a very rare and gifted
White Cat. At this the brothers laughed loudly and
exchanged pleased glances, for now they were convinced that he was indeed a simpleton and they
need have no fears of his outwitting them a third
time.

28

THE WHITE CAT

Through the streets of the city the two elder Princes rode with their ladies in open carriages, while the youngest Prince came last. Behind him was borne the great rock crystal, at which every one gazed in wonder.

The two Princes eagerly charged up the palace stairs with their Princesses, so anxious were they for their father's approval. The King received them graciously, but once more had difficulty in deciding which should have the prize. So he turned to his youngest son, who stood alone before him.

"Have you returned empty-handed this time?" he asked.

"In this rock your Majesty will find a little White Cat," he answered, "one which mews so sweetly and has such velvet paws that you cannot but be delighted with it."

But before the surprised King could reach the crystal, the Princess touched an inner spring. It flew open revealing her in all her beauty, more dazzling than the sun itself. Her hair fell in golden ringlets; she was crowned with flowers and she moved with incomparable grace in her gown of white and rose-colored gauze. Even the King himself could not resist such loveliness, but hastened to acknowledge her undisputed right to wear the crown.

"But I have not come to deprive your Majesty of a throne which you fill so admirably," she said, bowing before him graciously. "I was born the heiress to six kingdoms of my own, so permit me to offer one to you and to each of your elder sons. I ask no other favors of you than your friendship and that your youngest son shall be my husband. Three kingdoms will be quite enough for us."

And so in truth they found them.

GRACIOSA
AND PERCINET

GRACIOSA AND PERCINET

GRACIOSA was the only daughter of a King and Queen who loved her so dearly that to gratify her lightest wish meant more to them than the length and breadth of their kingdom. Each morning her mother presented her with a beautiful new dress of brocade or velvet or cloth of gold, and she could have sugar plums and sweetmeats at every meal. But in spite of all this she was not a proud Princess. Indeed, she was as good-hearted as she was charming to look upon, so it was no wonder

33

she was beloved of all the court and country.

Not quite by all, however, for a certain rich old Duchess named Groules began to be very jealous of her. It was not surprising, for Groules was as ugly and wicked as the Princess was lovely. She had hair as red as fire, only one eye, and a mouth

wide enough to swallow a whole regiment. Besides this she had a hump on her back and a different limp for each of her legs. Still, for all that, she persisted in believing herself beautiful and it infuriated her to hear a word of praise for Graciosa.

"It is false!" she would exclaim if any one so much as dared to mention the Princess's charms before her. "I have more beauty in my little finger than she has in her whole body!"

Now it happened that the good Queen fell ill and died, leaving Graciosa disconsolate and lonely.

GRACIOSA AND PERCINET

The King and all the court went into mourning for a twelvemonth, but at last the court physician persuaded the King to go out hunting in the hope of cheering his spirits. As luck would have it the chase ended near the château of Groules, who when she heard the horns and learned of the royal visitor,

hurried out to invite him to come in and partake of a little refreshment.

The King was very thirsty and tired, and gladly followed her into the cellar, where she begged him to choose his favorite wine. No sooner had he done so than she tapped the cask with a little hammer and out fell a shower of golden coins. On she went to another and another and always, when she tapped, gold or precious jewels poured out miraculously. It was her secret magic and the hammer possessed special power, but she pretended she

35

knew nothing of this and made a great many apologies to the King for giving him such trifles instead of wine.

The King's amazement grew and grew. His eyes became dazzled by the sight of so much gold and such glittering gems strewing the floor at his feet. Unfortunately the King had a great weakness for money, and when she made light of all this wealth he could not contain his admiration and desire to possess such a vast and inexhaustible supply.

"Trifles!" he echoed. "There is treasure enough here to buy ten more kingdoms."

"Well," she answered with all her cunning, "it is nothing to what is in all these other casks, and they shall all be yours if only you will marry me!"

"To-morrow, if you wish!" exclaimed the King, completely carried away by the sight before him.

"But I must make one condition," Groules went on, "I must have the same power over your daughter as if I were her own mother. She must obey my will and be left entirely in my hands."

"Agreed," said the King, and gave her his hand upon it.

Groules in turn presented him with the key to the treasure vault, chuckling to herself with secret joy to think of her own cunning.

When the King rode back to his palace, his daughter ran to meet him as was her custom. But

36

her joy in his return was soon turned to grief when he told her that he would wed the ugly Duchess on the morrow. All her pleas and tears were in vain. The King, who was now completely under Groules's evil influence, finally sent her away to her apartments, telling her to dress herself for the wedding and to remember hereafter that it was his command that she obey the new Queen as she had obeyed her own dead mother.

The poor Princess went weeping to her own room, where her old nurse begged to know the reason for her tears.

"Alas, dear Nurse," answered Graciosa, "who would not weep? The King is going to bring back my worst enemy to be my stepmother!"

"My dear child," replied the Nurse, "you must have a spirit as high and noble as your birth. Promise me, then, that you will not show your hatred of Groules."

So the Princess promised to put a good face on the matter and allowed the old nurse to dress her in her best for the wedding. In spite of her sadness she looked more beautiful than ever.

The ugly Duchess had attempted to beautify herself for the occasion by means of a glass eye and a black wig and by padding her dress to conceal the hump on her back. But this did not help matters much, even though in addition she put on a cloak of red and blue, a yellow petticoat trimmed with violet ribbons and as many other colors as she could think of.

Graciosa went into the garden to wait till she should be summoned to meet the wedding party. Here, alone and miserable, her tears fell so fast that she did not see a handsome young page approaching. He was all in green satin, with a feather on his hat, and he bowed low before her.

"Princess, the King awaits," he told her.

Graciosa was astonished at his looks and his charming manners, and when she asked how long he had been in her father's service, she was even more surprised to hear him answer:

"I am not the King's page. I am yours and will be yours only."

"Mine!" exclaimed the Princess in astonishment, "but I have never seen you before!"

"I dared not make myself known to you before," he told her; "but now that misfortune threatens you I could not remain silent any longer. I have come to declare my love to you."

"But you, a page!" cried Graciosa.

"That is how I appear now," he explained gently; "but really I am Percinet, a Prince, and already famous for my wealth and fairy magic. I have often watched you walking in these gardens and have loved you for a long time. At birth I was endowed with fairy power and I have come to put it at your service. To-day I will follow you every-

where in this page's habit to see that no harm befalls you."

"It is you then, handsome Percinet, of whom I have heard such strange stories told. I will no longer fear the wicked Groules, now that you have come to be my friend and protector."

A few more words passed between them. Then Graciosa followed him to the palace, where Percinet led forth a most beautiful and spirited horse which he had had put in the royal stables for her. Now the horse which had been selected for Groules to ride looked as clumsy as a farm nag beside Graciosa's. The Duchess saw this even with her one eye, a long way off, and her anger grew as she noticed the Princess's beauty and her handsome, green-clad page.

"Is this creature to have a finer horse than I?" cried Groules in a rage. "I shall return to my own castle at once if I am to be treated in such a manner."

The King, who had been too busy to notice this before, now ordered his daughter to dismount and give Groules her horse. When Graciosa had done so the Duchess was hoisted upon the spirited animal, where it took eight gentlemen to hold her.

Next she decided that the Green Page should hold the bridle as he had done when Graciosa rode it. Again the King ordered her wish to be gratified, and though the page and Graciosa exchanged a

look, Percinet took the reins in his hands. For a little, Groules was satisfied, and the procession set forth with trumpets and drums.

But suddenly, lo and behold, the fine horse began to bound, to rear and gallop at such a pace that no one could stop him. Groules clung to the saddle and to his mane, screaming with all her might. She fell off at last, one foot caught in the stirrup, so that she was dragged over stones and thorn bushes and finally into a great pile of mud and water. Never was bride in such a plight! They picked her up almost in pieces like a broken glass. They carried her into the city, put her to bed, and sent for the best doctors.

"Graciosa has played me this trick," she

stormed, ill as she was. "I'll see that she pays dearly for this or I will return to my own palace."

The King had now become so fearful of losing this wealth that he flew to her bedside upon hearing these threats and willingly agreed to any demands she might make, even those that concerned his only child.

So Graciosa was sent for, and this time there was no sign of the Green Page to cheer her. She had no sooner entered the invalid's room than four witches who served Groules seized the girl and at her command began tearing the clothes from the girl's back. But so white were her shoulders that the old women were nearly blinded and shut their

43

eyes as if they had been looking too long at snow. At this Groules cried out:

"Flay her till there is not a morsel left of that white skin she thinks so beautiful!"

So with brooms and birch rods they began to beat her without mercy while Groules urged them on from the bed. But the clever Percinet had so bewitched the eyes of these women that they believed they held rods in their hands while in reality they held only bunches of colored ostrich feathers. Seeing this, Graciosa ceased to be afraid, saying to herself: "Ah, Percinet, you have come to my aid once more. What should I have done without you?"

At last when they were too tired to inflict another blow, the four women bundled her into her cloak and turned her out of the room with a thousand abusive names. She returned to her own chamber and, pretending to be very ill, went to bed and ordered only her nurse to stay with her. To her she related her adventure, and what was her joy upon waking in an hour to behold the Green Page waiting in a corner of her apartment. She thanked him for his help and he renewed his promise to serve her.

Groules was so overjoyed to hear that the girl had taken to her bed that she recovered with all speed and her marriage to the King was celebrated with great magnificence. A tournament was arranged in honor of the day, which the royal family witnessed from a balcony hung with cloth-of-gold. Groules imagined that she was herself the center of all attention while in reality the beauty of Graciosa seated beside her drew all eyes in that direction.

At last, however, an unknown Knight appeared to challenge the beauty of Groules. He bore in his hands a jeweled box which he said held the portrait of the fairest maiden in the world. The six knights who wore Groules's colors advanced to meet his charge, but so great was his skill that he easily routed them all. He then opened the box, which contained the likeness of Graciosa herself. The victorious Knight then bowed low before her and disappeared without explaining his name or presence there. Graciosa had no doubt in her mind that this was Percinet in one of his many disguises.

Groules meantime had flown into a passion of jealous rage. In vain the Princess protested her innocence of any hand in the affair. Groules only raved like a madwoman, vowing that she would have vengeance or death. Some of the ladies-in-waiting became so alarmed that they ran to inform the King of his wife's fury and the Princess's terror. They implored him to have pity on Graciosa, for if the girl should be left to the mercy of the Queen she would certainly do her a thousand mischiefs. But he remained unmoved by the appeal.

The wicked Groules could scarcely wait for evening to come. As soon as it was dark she ordered her coach and horses, and into this she bundled Graciosa, giving directions to the escort that she should be taken to a forest not far off, a place so vast and full of savage beasts that none dared venture in it. In the midst of this wilderness they left her, though the poor Princess begged to be put to death immediately rather than left to such a fate. But the Queen's servants were deaf to her entreaties and galloped off, leaving her alone in the forest. For a time she tried to find some way out, but at last, exhausted with stumbling against trees and being caught in bushes, she threw herself down upon the ground in despair.

"Percinet!" she cried aloud, "Percinet! Where are you? Is it possible that you have abandoned me?"

She had scarcely uttered the words when her eyes were dazzled by a sudden flare of lights. Not a tree in the forest but bore a chandelier ablaze with wax tapers. At the far end of a long avenue she beheld a palace of shimmering crystal that shone like the sun itself. So bewildered was she, however, that when she heard a noise in the trees behind her she dared not look about but ran in the opposite direction. Presently she recognized Percinet's voice calling to her.

"Come, come without fear into the fairy palace!"

And Percinet was beside her, in a little golden

46

sledge drawn by two swans who bore it with incredible swiftness. Soon they were flying through the forest, Percinet introducing Graciosa to all sorts of delectable new sights. Here were shepherds and shepherdesses dancing to the music of flutes and bagpipes. In another spot vast fountains and singing youths and maidens.

"Once I thought this forest was uninhabited," cried Graciosa in wonder, "but now it seems filled with happy people."

"From the moment you set foot in it," Percinet told her, "this gloomy solitude has become filled with mirth and pleasure."

He then ordered the swans to take them to the palace, from which exquisite music sounded. A beautiful Queen and two charming Princesses ad-

47

vanced to meet them as the sledge drew up to the gate, and these Percinet introduced to her as his mother and sisters. They welcomed Graciosa most affectionately, leading her into the great entrance hall where to her surprise she saw all her own history painted upon the walls even up to the very moment of her rescue in the wood.

"You must have very diligent artists," observed Graciosa to Percinet, "for here is every action, every gesture, every expression of mine."

"Because I could not bear to lose the smallest one, my Princess," answered Percinet, gallantly.

That evening an opera was performed in Graciosa's honor which she watched from a beautiful little box made of ivory, lined in blue and festooned with roses. When this was over the Princess was led to her own apartments, more richly furnished than any she had ever seen. Here she was waited on by four-and-twenty maidens, dressed as nymphs, each one a marvel of beauty. In the morning she no sooner awoke than they brought her dresses of every fashion and color, jewelry of every design, besides laces, ribbons, gloves, and every sort of exquisite trinket imaginable. Never had she been so perfectly dressed; never had she looked so beautiful.

Percinet, still wearing his green livery, was overcome at sight of her. He implored her to marry him at once and remain in the palace forever. But

GRACIOSA AND PERCINET

Graciosa shook her head, for she was torn between her pleasure in being with Percinet in his beautiful palace and her duty to return to her father, whom she longed to save from the cruel clutches of Groules. At last, almost in spite of herself, she was persuaded to remain there for a week, during which time Percinet and his mother and sisters invented a thousand entertainments to please her.

"How I should like to know what is passing at my father's court," she said to Percinet one day, "and how Groules has explained my disappearance."

"Follow me into the high tower, then," he told her, "and you shall see for yourself."

So he led her to a tower all of rock crystal. Once they had reached the top he told her to link her little finger in his and then to look in the direction of the city. No sooner had she done so, than all that was taking place in the palace was spread plainly before her. She not only saw, but heard, the wicked Groules conversing with the King.

"That wretched daughter of yours has hanged herself in the cellar," she heard her telling him, "I have just seen her, and she is a fine sight indeed! But you will get over so trifling a loss once the funeral is over!"

At this news the King began to weep, for in spite of Groules he still had affection for his daughter. The Queen, seeing this, hurried away to her own apartments where she dressed a log of wood in one of Graciosa's old dresses and had it put into an elaborate coffin. There followed a grand funeral and all the court went into deep mourning. From the tower Graciosa could hear the lamentations for her loss, and all the people saying to one another: "What a pity that this lovely young Princess should perish through the cruelties of this wicked Queen." The King would neither eat nor drink and cried as if his heart were broken.

This sight so affected Graciosa that she also began to weep.

"Ah, Percinet, I cannot let my father believe that I am dead any longer. If you love me, then take me back to him."

In vain Percinet begged her to stay, but at last he could do nothing but yield to her pleas. So she took leave of his mother and sisters and seated herself beside him in the little sledge, behind the two swift swans. Away they sped and even as they glided through the shining gates a great noise sounded in their ears. Looking back Graciosa saw that the beautiful palace lay shattered into a thousand bright fragments. Frightened, Graciosa clung to Percinet.

"What is this that I see?" she cried. "Your palace is destroyed!"

"My palace is nothing now," replied he sadly, "since you are never to enter it again."

"Do not be angry with me, dear Prince," whispered the Princess, tears starting to her eyes. "Am I not more to be pitied than you?"

Percinet, by means of his magic powers, caused the sledge to be invisible. In this way he drove the Princess straight into her father's presence, where at first sight of his daughter he believed her to be a ghost. Once they were alone together, however, the Princess told of her stepmother's cruelty and of being abandoned to her fate in the great woods. She pretended, however, that she had taken refuge in a tall tree, living upon nuts and wild berries. The King listened amazed and when she told him of the log of wood that had been buried in her place, he could scarcely credit his ears. Indeed, he ordered the royal coffin to be opened at once, and sure enough there was the log all elaborately dressed in Graciosa's robes.

Any other King would have ordered the Queen out of the palace at once, but he had grown too weak to assert his authority; so he only kissed his daughter and bade her sit down to supper with him. Hearing this from her palace spies, Groules flew into a more terrible passion than before. She burst into the King's apartments and denounced Graciosa as an upstart and cheat, insisting that she scarcely resembled the dead Princess in a single feature and ending by saying that unless the King turned this impostor over to her immediately she would leave the palace, taking all her treasure with her. So completely had the King fallen under Groules's evil influence that he gave up the unfortunate Princess, believing, or pretending to believe, that she was not his daughter.

Now poor Graciosa was thrown ruthlessly into the deepest dungeon. They took away all her rich garments, giving her instead only a ragged cloak and hood, and rough wooden shoes. These, with a pile of straw to lie on, and a bit of black bread, were all she had. Alone in her distress the girl began to weep and regret the fairy palace she had so lately left. But she dared not call on Percinet for help, for she felt she had displeased him. She could not believe that he could love her enough to come to her aid again.

Meantime the wicked Queen had called to her aid a fairy only a little less cruel than herself.

"I have in my power a girl who has offended me," she explained, "and it is my desire to punish her with tasks so difficult that she will never be able to perform them. Help me to find a new torment for her every day till I am rid of her."

The cruel fairy agreed to this and was as good as her word. First she brought an enormous skein of thread so finely spun that a breath could break it and hopelessly tangled into a knotty snarl. This was flung down before the Princess in her dungeon cell while Groules explained with malicious smiles that if it were not all smoothly wound and untangled by sunset she would be flayed without mercy.

Graciosa took up the thread as carefully as possible, but before she had managed to undo one knot she had broken the strand in several places. At this she became more confused and finally aban-

55

doned all attempts at unraveling it. So, flinging the silken snarl into the middle of the floor, she buried her face in her hands and cried bitterly.

"Ah, Percinet, Percinet!" she sobbed. "If you still love me I implore you to come and take a last farewell of me before I die!"

At that the dungeon door opened as easily as if Percinet had had the key in his pocket.

"Here I am, dear Princess," he answered, hurrying to her side. "I only ask to be able to serve you."

With that he struck the skein of silk three blows with his magic wand and the broken strands immediately knitted themselves together, while two more touches unraveled the tangle perfectly. And not a moment too soon, for the sun was already dropping behind the horizon. Percinet had just time to make himself invisible before Groules appeared, eager to have her vengeance.

Once more the four witches who served her were in attendance. Groules smiled confidently at them as she unlocked the door, saying: "I'll wager now this idle beauty hasn't wagged one of her ten fingers." But she had no sooner entered than Graciosa advanced to hand her the silken ball. Dumbfounded at the sight, she could find no fault except to say that Graciosa had soiled it and to give her two smart slaps on either cheek. The Princess bore this so patiently that it only angered Groules the

56

more. She rushed away to her own apartments in order to concoct a still greater humiliation.

A second time she sent for the evil fairy and they put their two wicked old heads together to think up another cruel punishment, one that the girl could not possibly hope to escape. The fairy reappeared next day bringing with her a great barrel full of feathers. There were some from every sort of bird: from nightingales, canaries, greenfinches, goldfinches, linnets, redwings, parrots, owls, sparrows, doves, ostriches, peacocks, larks, and partridges—it would be impossible to name them all. These feathers were so mixed together that even the birds could not have told themselves apart!

"Here," said the fairy to Groules, "is something to try the skill and patience of your prisoner. Order her to pick out these feathers and put the peacock's, the nightingale's, and every other sort each by itself in a separate heap. It would be a task to try a fairy!"

Groules was ready to die of joy, picturing to herself the perplexity of the unhappy Princess. So she sent for her, threatened her as before, and shut her up with the barrel of feathers in a room with three locks, ordering her to finish her work by sunset if she did not wish to die.

Graciosa did try to pick out a few of the feathers, but she soon gave up the task as hopeless and fell to crying. "Let me die and end my misfortunes," she cried. "I will not again call Percinet to my aid. If he loved me he would have been here already."

"Here I am, my Princess," exclaimed he, rising out of the barrel in which he had concealed himself, "come to save you. After so many proofs of my affection can you doubt that I love you more than myself?"

Thereupon he gave the barrel three taps with his wand and the feathers came out by the million, sorting themselves into neat heaps all round the room.

"What do I not owe you, dear Percinet!" cried the grateful Princess. "But for you I should have perished!"

Groules now approached, and her wrath knew no bounds at finding Graciosa alone in the cell and surrounded by the skillfully sorted feathers. So, in spite of taking some little satisfaction out of giving the girl a sound beating, she returned to her apartments and once again summoned the fairy. This time she upbraided her for not having found a task too difficult for the Princess's skill. But the wicked fairy promised to make a box which should bring great trouble upon whosoever should open it.

A few days afterward she returned carrying a box which Groules immediately ordered to be sent to Graciosa with directions that she should carry it to Groules's castle in the distant woods, and that she must not open it on pain of death.

So Graciosa set off in her wooden shoes, her coarse woolen dress and hood, like a little peasant, though nothing could completely conceal her marvelous beauty. She had not walked far before she began to feel very tired. She happened to be passing through a little wood on the outskirts of a pleasant meadow where she sat down to rest herself. She placed the box across her two knees, and as she stared at it a great longing came upon her to open it.

"What can happen to me," she thought, "if I take only one little look inside?"

So without thinking of the consequences she lifted the lid. Immediately out trooped a company of tiny men and women, all carrying fiddles and other musical instruments, and little tables and chairs and miniature dishes. The tallest one of these little creatures was no bigger than her smallest finger. They skipped about the meadow, dividing themselves into groups. Some began to dance the prettiest steps that ever were seen; others played on horns and fiddles, while still others cooked and others feasted. It was all enchanting, and at first Graciosa looked on amazed at so extraordinary a sight. But once she felt rested and wished to get them all safely into the box again, not one would obey her. All the little gentlemen and ladies ran away. The fiddlers followed their example. The cooks scampered off to the woods with their pots and stew pans over their shoulders. Though she pursued them round and round the meadow and through the trees, she could never catch so much as a flying coat-tail or an elf-lock.

She was in despair.

"Oh, Percinet!" she cried. "Percinet! Come and help me!"

Percinet did not wait to be called twice. Instantly he was before her in his green page's dress. Once again he tapped the box with his wand and all the little men and women, fiddles, tables, chairs, dishes and tiny roasts of meat were all packed into the box as neatly as if they had never been out of it.

Percinet had left his coach in the wood, and Graciosa was only too delighted to accept his offer to drive her to the castle, for she was quite spent with all her anxious runnings to and fro. He made them both invisible, but once they arrived at Groules's castle the Princess resumed her own form, still clad in the rags in which her stepmother had sent her on this journey. Knocking at the gate, she demanded entrance in the name of Groules. But the steward would not listen to her, believing her to be some upstart of a peasant girl. She at last persuaded him to write his refusal on a bit of paper as proof that she had really reached the doors of the castle.

With this in hand she returned to the edge of

the wood, where the faithful Percinet was waiting for her. But when she asked him to drive her over to her father's palace he began to beg her not to fall once again into Groules's clutches.

"Why should you be subjected to such misery," he said, "when one little word from you can bring us joy forever and ever?"

"I must return with the box to prove my innocence," she answered. "Who knows but this time Groules's heart may be softened and I may once more know my father's love?"

In vain did Percinet plead with her. Graciosa's mind was made up.

"But if my stepmother tricks me once more, I agree to marry you without further delay," she told him.

Percinet was forced to content himself with this promise, and reluctantly he watched her enter the palace alone.

When Groules saw her returning her fury was more terrible than it had ever been before. She threw the box and the letter into the fire and indeed she would have flung the Princess after them if she had dared. This time she did not send for the fairy, but took matters into her own hands. She had a great hole dug in the garden and a stone rolled over this. She then took Graciosa for a walk there with her. As they approached the place she pointed to the stone and remarked: "I have been told that

63

great treasure is buried beneath this. Let us lift it away quickly." Unsuspectingly Graciosa lent a helping hand. Once the stone was rolled aside it was an easy matter for Groules to push the Princess over the edge into the deep pit and then to cover it again as if nothing had happened.

Poor Graciosa, trapped and miserable in the darkness at the bottom of the pit, felt that this time the case was quite hopeless. Tears came to her eyes as she remembered Percinet and all his loving words. With all her heart she wished that she had heeded his warnings and had married him without returning to such a fate.

"Ah, dear Percinet," she sobbed, "if only I had listened to you I should not now be buried alive. I should be happy with you in a fairy palace, not facing a cruel death here in the bottom of the earth."

Suddenly through her tears she saw a little door near by. It opened upon sunshine and gardens filled with flowers, fruits, and splashing fountains. She did not hesitate to step across the threshold, her eyes round with wonder that had so lately been wet with weeping. At the far end of a green avenue of trees stood the fairy palace, more beautiful than ever, and as if it had never crumbled away before her eyes. And here was Percinet advancing to meet her with his mother and sisters beside him.

"You can refuse my son no longer, sweet Princess," smiled the Queen. "The time has come for you to make Percinet happy and to free yourself from the tyranny of Groules."

Graciosa's thankfulness was such that she fell on her knees before the Queen, saying that she placed her fate entirely in her hands and that she would obey her in all things. The Queen then told her of an ancient prophecy which had said she should not reënter the fairy palace until after she had been buried in the ground. Now that the prophecy had been fulfilled and all the evil spells broken, there was no reason to delay the marriage longer.

With tears of joy and gratefulness the Princess gave Percinet her hand. She could not give him her heart, for he had had that ever since the day of their first meeting in her father's garden. Percinet, in his turn, knelt at her feet, while the whole palace rang with music and singing.

Only good fairies were invited to attend the wedding and they came from a thousand leagues

65

round in the most amazing equipages. Some were in cars drawn by swans, by fireflies, or by dragons; others on clouds, on stars, or in globes of fire. So the marriage of Graciosa and Percinet was celebrated. Never has there been its like, before or since.

THE
POT OF CARNATIONS

THE POT OF CARNATIONS

THERE was once a poor man who called his son and daughter to his deathbed in order that he might divide his property between them. He had very little to leave, but he wished to make sure there should be no dispute after he was gone. To his son he gave his furniture and livestock, and this amounted to two joint stools, a mattress, and a hen.

69

THE WHITE CAT

For his daughter there remained only a plain silver ring and a pot of carnations. These, he told her, had been given to him by a great lady who had once lived in his hut.

"My good man," she had said to him at parting, "here is a present I shall make you. Be careful to lock the ring in a safe place and to water the plant each day and your daughter shall be the most beautiful girl in the world. Name her Fortunée, for the ring and carnations will console her for her poverty, and bring her good fortune."

Neither Fortunée nor her brother Bedou made any dispute over their inheritance, and for some time after their father's death they continued to live on in contentment together in the little hut. Fortunée never doubted that her brother loved her till one day when she happened to be seated on one of the stools, he turned upon her fiercely.

"Keep your carnations and your ring," he cried, "but do not touch my stools! I will not have the furniture disturbed in my house!"

Fortunée began to weep silently, but being far too gentle to cause a dispute, she remained standing while her brother sat on one stool with his feet on the other. At supper Bedou had a fine new-laid egg from his hen. When he was through, he hurled the shell at his sister.

"There," he said, "I have nothing else to give you. If you are not satisfied, go out and hunt for frogs. You will find plenty in the marshes round-about!"

Fortunée made no answer but once more tears filled her eyes. This time she went to her own room, which suddenly seemed full of the sweetest perfume. This, she felt sure, must come from the pot of carnations, so she drew nearer and spoke to it sadly.

"Beautiful carnations," she whispered, "you who console my heart by your sweet perfume, do not fear that I shall ever let you want for water or tear you from your stems. I shall cherish you, for you are my only treasures."

She had no sooner finished speaking than she noticed that the plant was very dry, so she took her pitcher and hastened out in the moonlight to fetch fresh water. The fountain was some distance away and when she reached it Fortunée sat down beside it to rest herself.

But she had scarcely been there a moment before she saw a magnificent Lady approaching her, surrounded by a company of gayly clad attendants. Six maids of honor carried her train, while two others walked on her either side. Her guards moved before her, dressed in green and carnation-colored satin, embroidered in gold. Between them they bore an armchair, covered in cloth of gold. The Lady seated herself in this presently. Then the attendants raised a rich canopy over her head and spread the most delicious feast before her. Fortunée still stood a little apart, marveling at all she saw. In a few moments the Lady turned to one of her train and said: "Is that a shepherdess I see near the thicket? Let her approach."

Hearing this, Fortunée gathered courage to draw nearer. In spite of her unhappiness and timidity she none the less made such a graceful curtsy that all who saw her were astonished. She kissed the hem of the great Lady's robe, and then stood before her with flushed cheeks and downcast eyes.

"What are you doing here, pretty girl?" asked the Lady. "Are you not afraid to be in this lonely spot so late at night?"

"Alas," replied Fortunée, "why should I fear? What have I that any robber should notice?"

"You are not rich then, my child?"

"Madam," replied Fortunée, "I am as poor as this: my father left me only a silver ring and a pot of carnations."

"But you have a Heart," persisted the Lady, "and if any one wished for that, would you give it away?"

"I do not know what it is to give my Heart," the girl answered wonderingly. "I have always understood that without a Heart we could not live, that if it should be wounded we must die; and in spite of my poverty I am not sorry to be alive."

"You are quite right to feel so about your Heart, my child. But tell me, have you had a good supper to-night?"

The Queen of the Fountain

THE POT OF CARNATIONS

"No, madam," replied Fortunée, "because my brother ate it all."

The Lady then commanded that a place be laid for her, and that the girl be seated and helped to the best food. But Fortunée was so lost in admiration of the great Lady's beauty and so touched by her goodness, that she could scarcely eat a morsel.

"I am very anxious to know," continued her hostess, "what brought you so late to this lonely fountain?"

"Madam," she answered, "I came to fetch water for my carnations. See, here is my pitcher."

She stooped to pick it up and as she did so perceived to her amazement that instead of her old brown earthenware one, the pitcher was of pure gold, crusted with diamonds, and filled with deliciously perfumed water. She dared not touch it, thinking it could not be hers. But the Lady with a gracious gesture bid her take it.

"I give it to you, Fortunée," she said. "Go home and water your flowers and always remember that the Queen of the Fountain is your friend."

The girl flung herself at the other's feet, begging her to remain there till she could return to the hut, for she wished to give her the pot of carnations in token of her gratefulness. So, taking her golden pitcher, she ran to her little room. But during her absence Bedou had entered, taken away her pot of carnations, and left in their place a large cabbage. Poor Fortunée was in despair. At first she almost decided not to return to the fountain, but thinking better of this, she ran back to her benefactress.

"Oh, madam," she cried, throwing herself upon her knees before her, "Bedou has taken my flowers. Now I have only my ring. I hope you will accept that instead as proof of my gratitude."

"If I take your ring, my dear," replied the Queen of the Fountain, "you will have nothing left."

"Ah," answered the girl, "that could never be while I have your good opinion."

So the Queen of the Fountain took the ring, put it upon her finger, and then seated herself in a coach of coral and emeralds, drawn by six white horses more beautiful than the steeds of the sun. Fortunée stood gazing after it as long as she could see. But at last a turn in the road hid it from her sight and she returned to Bedou's cottage, her eyes still dazzled by her adventure.

Her first act upon entering her own room was to throw the cabbage out of the window. But she had no sooner done so than she was astonished to hear a voice cry: "Oh, I am killed!" Fortunée was at a loss what to make of this, for she knew that as a rule cabbages do not speak. When it was daylight, she arose and went out into the garden. Here as she searched for her pinks, what should she see but the unfortunate cabbage. As she passed, she

76

thrust it aside with her foot, saying: "Why did you dare to take the place of my beloved carnations?"

"If I had not been carried it would never have entered my head to go there," replied the cabbage.

Again Fortunée trembled to hear it speak, but the cabbage continued to address her.

"If you will carry me back to my companions," it said, "I will tell you that your carnations are hidden in Bedou's straw mattress."

This only distressed Fortunée the more, for she had no idea how to recover them, but she picked up the cabbage and started for the other end of the garden. As she did so she stumbled upon her brother's hen.

"So you, too, would cause me trouble!" she exclaimed with displeasure, for she had very nearly fallen over it.

The little hen was in such a flutter of fright that it ruffled its feathers and set up a great cackling. Suddenly Fortunée realized that the hen was also speaking to her, though its voice was somewhat indistinct owing to extreme fear and lack of breath. But presently she began to make out the words that the little white hen was trying to say.

"The time has now come, my dear Fortunée," it said, "to tell you some wonderful things. Do not imagine that you are really the child of the poor woodsman who brought you up. You are the youngest daughter of a great and good Queen who was forced to flee from her country and her castle,

because her cruel husband threatened death to their child unless it should be a son and heir. Her half-sister, a good fairy, tried to intervene and exchange you for her own baby son, but it was too late. One of the castle guards allowed the Queen to escape and she fled to this lonely cottage in the woods. I was the wife of the poor man you believed to be your father, and when the Queen arrived, nearly dead with grief and fatigue, I cared for her as best I could. She told me her misfortunes and gave you into my charge, but she was too weak to tell me what I should do with a royal baby.

78

THE POT OF CARNATIONS

"Unfortunately I have always been a great gossip. I could not resist telling every one about this strange adventure. One day a beautiful Lady in rich dress came to our door and I told her also the whole story. When I had finished she touched me with a wand she carried and instantly I became what you see me now, a white hen, without power to speak, only able to scratch and dig in the garden that I had once tended so carefully. Imagine my grief and humiliation! My husband was away at work in the wood, and when he returned he looked everywhere for me, though I was there beneath his very feet. Finally he gave up searching, believing that I had been drowned or devoured by wild beasts.

"Once more this great Lady who had cast the spell over me passed by, and this time she ordered my husband to call you Fortunée and she also gave him the silver ring and the pot of carnations. But just as she was taking her leave, five and twenty armed soldiers appeared at the door. They had been sent by the King, your father, who had been warned of your hiding place. Knowing well that they sought you for some evil purpose, our visitor changed them in a twinkling into green cabbages. They are growing there in a corner of the garden. Indeed it was one of them that you threw out of your window last night. I have never heard them speak before, but for that matter I have never been able to regain my voice until this moment."

"My poor nurse!" cried Fortunée, who was filled with sympathy at the tale. "To think that you

should have to be a hen! And all because of me! I would so gladly restore you to your own form if it were in my power to do so. But you must not despair, for now that you have told me the true state of affairs, things cannot remain so forever. I shall go now and look for my dear carnations."

So saying, Fortunée ran to the cottage and into her brother's room. She would not have dared to enter it had she not already seen him set off to hunt in the forest. But no sooner was she in it than a huge army of rats gathered all about the mattress. So terrifying was their appearance that the poor girl had not the courage to go near them. She was determined, however, that they should not harm her carnations, and she began to think how she might outwit them. Suddenly it occurred to her that the perfumed water in the golden vase she had carried home the night before might have some peculiar power. She ran to fetch it and immediately a drop touched one of the rats, it scurried back into its hole, leaving Fortunée free to rescue her carnations from under the bed.

The flowers were drooping and sadly in need of water, so she poured all that remained in her pitcher on their parched roots. Even as she did so, she heard a sweet voice speaking from among the stalks.

"Dear Fortunée," it said, "at last the day I have wished for has come when I may tell you of my love, for your beauty and goodness are so great that even flowers must be moved to love you."

Fortunée could scarcely believe her ears! First to hear a cabbage, then a hen, and now a carnation, speak! In fact she was so startled that she fell into a faint and was only roused when her brother returned and rudely flung her out of doors. But here at the edge of the forest she was not long left alone.

Almost instantly the beautiful Queen of the Fountain stood beside her.

"You have indeed a bad brother, my child," she said. "I saw his treatment of you just now with my own eyes. Tell me, shall I avenge his cruelty?"

But Fortunée was too kind to bear him any malice. At this the Queen was secretly pleased, and went on to talk of the great difference between these two children of the poor woodcutter, asking the girl if she were sure that Bedou were really her own brother.

"Have you never heard that you were born a Princess?" she asked at last.

Fortunée hung her head and replied shyly that she had but lately heard such a rumor.

"But," she added modestly, "how can I boast of something of which I have no proof to offer? How am I to be certain that I am more than a poor woodcutter's daughter?"

At these words the Lady smiled upon her even more approvingly, for she was delighted to see that the girl's head was in no danger of being turned by any change of fortune.

"Nevertheless, you are a Princess," she told her, "though it has not been in my power to save you from the misfortunes you have suffered up to this hour."

At this moment they were interrupted by the appearance of a young man more beautiful than

the day. He wore robes of gold and green, thickly bejeweled, and his head was crowned with carnations. Bending before the Queen of the Fountain, he saluted her respectfully. She in her turn embraced him with deepest affection.

"Welcome, my dear son!" she cried. "The time of your fatal enchantment is ended at last, thanks to the aid of Fortunée." And turning to the bewildered girl she continued: "Sweet Princess, I know all that the hen told you. But what you do not know is that my dear son here, who was to have been exchanged for you in infancy, was turned by the spell of a wicked fairy with whom I had quarreled, into a carnation. All my magic was of no avail until I thought to bring Prince Carnation, safe in his flower pot, to the cottage where your mother the Queen had left you. I could foresee that a day would come when you would sprinkle the flowers with the enchanted water from the golden pitcher, and that then he would speak; he would love you and thereafter nothing more would mar your happiness. Once you had given me the silver ring I knew that the time had come when the spell would be over. If you return my son's love, you two shall be married with this very ring and your happiness will last forever."

At this Fortunée's cheeks grew as pink as the wreath of carnations.

"Ah, madam," she stammered, "you overwhelm

85

me with favors. But how can I, a girl brought up in poverty and loneliness, be sure of his Heart, though I confess that for the first time in my life I feel I could not be happy without his love!"

"Be assured on that point, sweetest Princess," cried Prince Carnation, "did I not declare my devotion to you even when I was rooted to my flower pot?"

The Queen of the Fountain now insisted that Fortunée must have clothes more fitting to her new station in life, so she touched the rough cotton dress and immediately it was changed into cloth of silver, embroidered with precious gems. On her hair a crown of coral pink carnations was set, with pearls and diamonds sparkling on the petals like drops of dew. Her cheeks grew more dazzlingly pink and white as the Prince stood marveling at her beauty and his own good fortune. As the three turned to go to the Queen's palace, who should appear but Bedou returning from work. Seeing his sister arrayed like a Goddess of Beauty, he rubbed his eyes in amazement. At sight of him, Fortunée called out a kindly greeting and begged the Queen to have pity on him.

"What, after the way he ill-treated you!" she exclaimed in surprise.

"But, madam," replied the girl, "my own happiness is so great that I cannot bear him any ill will."

"It shall be as you wish," the Queen promised, kissing Fortunée and praising her generosity. "For your sake the ungrateful Bedou shall be rewarded."

She was as good as her word and presently the poor woodcutter's hut turned into a fine palace,

and only his two wooden stools and his old mattress remained unchanged to be a reminder and a warning to him. Not only did the Queen effect this change in his surroundings, but she proceeded to improve his manners and appearance as well. Suddenly Bedou found himself full of a new feeling. This was gratitude, a sensation he had never experienced before in his life! His own surprise at the strange words he found himself saying was even more than that of his three listeners.

Finally, by a stroke of the Queen's magic wand, the cabbages became men once more and the white hen a woman, who was the happiest person of all at the wedding of Fortunée and Prince Carnation.

She would not, however, consent to live with them in the royal palace, but asked for a little cottage of her own with a garden. This, she explained, was because her long years of being a hen had given her a taste for the soil, and she spent hours there, digging contentedly from force of habit!

PRINCE SPRITE

PRINCE SPRITE

ONCE upon a time there were a King and a Queen who loved their only son more than anything else in the world although he was ugly in mind and body. Indeed, he was so distorted and uncouth that the meanest toad would have seemed charming in comparison. But the ugliness of his face and the deformity of his body were nothing compared to the cruelty of his disposition. He was an obstinate little beast who took delight in making every one about him miserable. The King had noticed this and had been worried by it even in the Prince's babyhood, but the Queen doted upon him and made matters worse by never denying him the

smallest wish. It was only too plain that he had her completely in his power. Realizing this, the members of the court soon fell into the habit of praising him, calling him handsome and clever, for only in this way could they hope to win the Queen's favor. Since no ordinary name was good enough for such a Prince, according to his mother, months of time and thought and study went into the choosing of a suitable one. At last she decided upon Furibon as one which was worthy of his rank and title.

PRINCE SPRITE

Now the time came for Furibon to have a tutor, and this presented a new problem for the King. Wishing his son to be in the best possible company, he at last decided upon a Prince who possessed

great charm and intelligence rather than wealth, although as a matter of fact he could boast a distant claim to the throne. This, however, was not considered a matter of much importance, since his father's estates had fallen into decay and the youth's only inheritances were his good looks, his quick wits, and his ability to please every one he met. In short this young Leander was the exact opposite of his royal companion in every way.

Naturally Furibon only seemed more hideous

by contrast when he and Leander appeared together, and by this time he was so spoiled that a hundred floggings could not have cured him of a single fault. Leander was a favorite wherever he went, especially with the court ladies, who all tried to win his favor, but without marked success. For though he was courteous toward all, he remained aloof and reserved in his manners, so that behind his back they sighed and deplored his indifference. Furibon, on the other hand, never missed an opportunity to treat some lady with rudeness.

No one in the palace escaped, from the humblest scullery maid to the most aristocratic Grand Duchess. All were one in their dread and dislike of him. And the more Furibon saw this the more he heaped his resentment on Leander.

"If the courtiers treated me with the smiles and familiarity they do you," the ugly little beast would sneer, "I would beat them all into a jelly for it!"

So matters went from bad to worse till it happened that two foreign ambassadors meeting the Prince and his companion, mistook Leander for the Heir to the Throne and supposed the other to be his dwarf. Accordingly they teased Furibon, and Leander could not make them understand the mistake they were making. It was no use, they did not speak the same language, so they continued to laugh heartily at Furibon's antics, for he had become almost beside himself with rage. Indeed, he

94

drew his sword and would have killed the two, had not the King intervened in the nick of time. After this, the Prince flew at his companion and would have killed him, too, if he had been the stronger. Leander was well able to defend himself, but his father, hearing of this insulting treatment, sent for his son to return to their château in the country.

Leander was glad to be back in his old haunts after the life at court and to amuse himself once more with hunting, fishing, and walking. In spite of the solitude of the place he never felt a moment's loneliness, for when he no longer cared for sport there were his books and his musical instruments.

One day, when the sun was particularly hot, he took refuge in the shade of a little wood where he began to amuse himself by playing on his flute. Suddenly in the midst of his tune he felt something twining about his leg. Looking down, he was surprised to see a large adder.

As he lifted his hand to kill it, the snake fixing him with its eyes seemed to beg for mercy. Just at this moment a gardener ran up to strike it down, but Leander held him off, for the adder, which was spotted with more rare and changing colors than he had ever seen before, still gazed at him strangely without making any effort to defend itself.

"It has come to me for protection," he said to the gardener, "and I forbid you to do it any harm.

95

I shall feed it and when it sheds this beautiful skin I will let it go again."

So he carried it back to the château and locked it into a room with plenty of fruit and herbs and flowers to feed upon. A lucky adder indeed! Sometimes he paid it visits, and on such occasions the snake would glide to meet him with all the best airs and graces an adder can muster. All this amused its protector, but he attached little importance to it.

This was not surprising for about this time his old trouble-maker, Furibon, played another malicious trick upon him. Prompted by his mother's advice, he arranged to join Leander for hunting in some near-by woods. Once he had him completely at his mercy he planned to give the signal for some of his attendants to attack and kill him. Eager and willing to forget all the unpleasant encounters he had had with the Prince in the past, Leander accepted the invitation. Fortunately, however, the attendants had no sooner surrounded him than a fierce lion appeared, scattering them in every direction, so that Leander was left to defend the Prince. This he did, but when the danger was past and Furibon still continued to heap insults upon him, Leander brought him back to his bodyguard, and sadly returned home.

He realized now that the Prince was his enemy and would try other means of killing him if he remained there. So at length he decided that the only course open to him was to leave the country. He would go abroad and see the world. But he must see the adder, and give it food and release it, before starting on his travels. He had no sooner unlocked the door than he noticed a curious light shining in one corner of the room. What was his great astonishment then to behold there a lady, whose grace and beauty left no doubt of her noble birth. Her dress was of shimmering satin, bordered with diamonds and pearls, and she advanced to meet him with a smile.

"Young Prince," said she, "do not look for the adder you saved from death. You see me in its place, waiting to repay the debt of gratitude it owes you." Then, as Leander showed how great was his bewilderment, she continued: "Know that I am the fairy Gentille. I come of a race that can live a hundred years without growing old, without illness, or fear or pain. At the end of that time we must become adders for the space of a single week. Only then are we in any danger, for if we are killed during those seven short days we can never come to life again. Once the week is over we return to our true shapes, but with greater beauty and power, and more treasures than before. You can well understand, my Lord, the gratefulness I feel toward you for saving me from such a fate. I shall do all in my power to repay this debt. You have only to speak and I shall call upon my magic to come to your aid."

"Madam," he answered, bowing low before her, "I ask nothing more than to have been of some slight service to you."

"Do not put me aside so carelessly," she insisted, "remember that I have the power to prolong your life, to make you a great king, to give you untold wealth, and even to make you a spirit of air or earth or water."

"But what possible use would that be to me?" asked Leander, wonderingly.

"You could do a thousand things you do not dream of now," she told him. "You could become invisible whenever you pleased. You could travel the universe in an instant's time. You could go to the center of the earth or the bottom of the sea at

Prince Sprite

will. In short you might enter any door or window, no matter how fast it might be barred to the rest of the world."

At this Leander's eyes grew very bright.

"I will be a spirit then," he exclaimed. "I prefer that above all the gifts you have so generously offered me."

"Be a spirit then," she said, passing her hand three times over his eyes, "but always a friendly and frolicsome one." So she christened him "Prince Sprite."

Next she handed him a little red hat ornamented with two parrot feathers. Leander could scarcely wait to try its power. The moment he clapped it on his head and wished to visit a distant wood to pick some wild roses—he found himself there. As miraculously, he was returned to his château almost before he was aware of having wished it. Charmed with this little trial trip, he presented the fairy with the roses he had gathered. But three of these she gave back to him. telling him that one would provide him with all the money he desired; the second, if placed above the heart of his true love, would assure him of her loyalty, while the third would preserve him from all sickness. Then, without waiting for thanks, the fairy Gentille wished him a fortunate journey and disappeared.

Now almost the first thing that occurred to Leander was that his new gift would enable him to play some tricks upon Furibon in exchange for all the torments he had endured in his days at court. So, mounting his favorite horse named Graylocks, and taking a small band of faithful servants, he set off for court with a light heart.

Meantime Furibon had spread abroad all sorts of tales of Leander's treachery to him in the hunt, and the Queen had given orders that if he even showed his face near the palace he should be thrown into the dungeons. News of Leander's approach therefore set the court in a great flutter and Furibon, who was above all things a coward, ran to his mother's apartments, for he dared not face his old comrade alone. So the Queen hastened to the King's council chamber to champion her son's cause and Furibon, eager to know what was happening behind the closed door, leaned against it with his ear close to the keyhole.

PRINCE SPRITE

Leander had on his little red cap, so no one saw him enter the grand hall of the palace. As soon as he spied the Prince and saw that he was up to his old trick of eavesdropping, he took up a hammer

and nail and nailed his ear to the doorpost. Furibon howled with pain and fear and pounded on the door like a madman. His mother, hurrying to answer his calls, flung open the door to let him in and in so doing pulled off his ear. Bleeding and making hideous grimaces, he flew about in a rage till the Queen sat him in her lap, picked up his ear, kissed it, and stuck it on again.

Next Leander took a handful of twigs and began to rap the Queen's knuckles and the Prince's nose with them smartly. The Queen cried that she was being murdered, the King stared and the attendants rushed in to find the assassin. Since there was no one to be seen, the rumor soon spread about that the Queen had lost her wits with worrying over Furibon's torn ear. The King himself began to believe these tales and fled when the Queen approached him.

By this time Leander felt satisfied with his revenge, so he returned to his waiting servants, distributed money among them and sent them back to the château again, for he had no wish to have followers who knew the secret of his little red hat and the roses. Then he mounted Graylocks once more and set off to follow whatever road took his fancy.

Adventure upon adventure followed, too numerous to tell, till at last he came to a deep and ancient forest where he could hear plainly the cries of a girl. In the distance he saw four men carrying off a young girl between them.

PRINCE SPRITE

"Is this maid a slave that you should treat her so?" he cried out, angrily.

But they only answered him with sneers, "What is that to you?"

"Release her instantly!" he commanded. But he might as well have talked to the trees, for all the satisfaction he got.

Once more it was time for the little red hat to come to his aid. He put it on and rode hot haste after them. The robbers stopped, once they supposed he had fled, leaving only one of their band to guard the prisoner. Soon Leander was standing near the young girl, listening to her sobs and cries.

"Alas, my beautiful Princess," she cried, "if

you guessed my misfortune you would send help to me!"

At that Leander seized the arm of the robber who held her and bound him to a tree. His cries brought the others, and one by one the invisible Prince beat and bound them, all the while teasing them with bits of talk and snatches of song. While this skirmishing was going on the girl made her escape, running wildly this way and that, for she had no idea how to get out of the forest. Presently Leander overtook her as she leaned exhausted against a tree, spent with her running. He had forgotten to remove his hat, and as he advanced with Graylocks he heard the girl cry out delightedly, "Good, good! Here is a fine horse that will carry Abricotine back to the Palace of Pleasures." Smiling to himself, the Prince lifted her up to the saddle before him and rode away with her.

Oh, what a fright she was in, to feel herself in the grasp of somebody and yet to see no one!

Even when Leander tried to pop a sweetmeat between her lips she would not open them, so at last he doffed his cap and spoke to her kindly.

"Why, Abricotine," said he, "how can you be so afraid of me when I am the one who rescued you just now from the hands of the robbers?"

"Oh, my Lord," she answered opening her eyes at the sound of his voice, "I am full of gratefulness toward you, but I feared to find myself in the power of an invisible being."

PRINCE SPRITE

Leander reassured her, and began asking her all manner of questions about herself, her age, her country, and the mischance that had let her fall into the hands of the robber band. And she promised to tell him the whole story if he would see that they never for a moment slackened their speed as they rode out of the wood.

"To begin with," she told him, "one of the most gifted of all the fairy race so far forgot her rank as to fall in love with a human being. He was a certain well-known Prince, whom she persisted in marrying against all the entreaties of the other fairies. They knew that this act would remove her from them forever and they warned her that she would find no true happiness in such a marriage. This proved true enough, for the Prince soon tired of his fairy wife, whose uncanny knowledge of magic and future events made him exceedingly uneasy. At last he treated her so cruelly that she took her infant daughter with her and transported her palace to a distant island, which she christened THE ISLE OF PEACEFUL PLEASURES. Here she allowed no man to set foot, and so great was her bitterness against the race that had caused her such misery, that she brought her young daughter up to shun the thought oi all men. A company of Amazonian women, all strong and skillful in every form of sport, served her and still care for the Princess, who is now the sole ruler of the Island, since she became of age and her mother returned to Fairyland. She

107

is the most beautiful creature in the world, and the most charming and gracious as well. I could wish for no greater joy than to continue forever in her service."

" 'Forever' is a word that comes lightly to the lips of the very young," Leander smiled as he spurred his horse on to greater speed.

But the charming Abricotine only laughed at his words.

"No one grows old in the Princess's palace," she answered. "I may look youthful but I am really more than two hundred years old."

When he had recovered from his surprise at this, she continued her tale, explaining how she had come to fall into the hands of the robbers. "So many have heard of the Princess's beauty and her portrait has traveled to such far regions, that Princes are constantly seeking to reach the Island to catch a glimpse of her and to woo her in marriage. We must therefore be very watchful lest some man find his way into the palace. My duties are to care for the royal birds, and one day I accidentally let her favorite parrot escape. Fearing her displeasure, I foolishly left the Island in search of it. I had scarcely set foot on the other shore when those ruffians seized me and carried me away. From their talk I learned that they were sent to spy upon the Princess and capture her for their Prince, an ugly misshapen fellow named Furibon who has fallen in love with her portrait. I do not know what my fate would have been if you had not come to my rescue."

"Then may I not be allowed to set foot upon this wonderful Island, and gaze upon this beautiful Princess who never grows old?" he asked her.

But she shook her head at this. "Ah, my Lord," said she, "we should be lost, both of us, if we attempted such a thing."

Leander continued to beg that he be admitted, and conversing in this manner they came at last to the bank of the river which separated the Isle of Peaceful Pleasures from the rest of the world. Abricotine sprang lightly to the ground.

"Farewell, my Lord," she said, making him a low curtsy. "I wish you so much happiness that the whole world shall be to you an island of pleasures. Hasten away, I beg you, before any of the ladies of the palace catch sight of you."

He in his turn charged her to keep him in her remembrance, and so they parted. But no sooner was he out of sight and in a wood by the river than he put on his little red hat and wished himself on the Isle of Peaceful Pleasures. Instantly he found himself in the most beautiful and rare palace he had ever seen.

It was built of pure gold with statues of clearest crystal about the parapets. These figures represented signs of the zodiac, and all creatures of the earth, air, and water. There were also scenes depicting Diana hunting with her nymphs, Amazons performing astounding feats of strength and skill, shepherdesses with their flocks, and other charming groups. But what amazed the Prince most of all was that among all these figures not one was a man.

"Abricotine told me the truth," said Leander to himself. "The very idea of man is banished from this spot."

Under cover of his invisibility he passed from room to room, encountering groups of pretty, laughing girls at every turn. Some of the apartments he found filled with the rarest china, others with flowers and fruits and the most delicious perfumes. In some the walls were transparent so that the light streamed through clearly, while others were of rock crystal, amber, coral, lapis-lazuli and carnelian. The Princess's own private apartment was entirely of looking-glass, as if it were impossible to multiply her charming person too often. A single enormous pearl had been hollowed into the shape of a sea-shell to form her throne, with precious rubies, diamonds, and emeralds festooning it in clusters. But they were as nothing beside the rare beauty of the Princess herself.

The Prince looked in vain for a single fault in her form and features. Her eyes were marvelously

soft and brilliant and her smile of enchanting love
liness. Hearing her questioning her ladies-in-wait·
ing as to what had become of her favorite Abricotine, Leander could contain himself no longer. Assuming the high, small voice of one of the parrots
hanging in near-by cages, he answered: "Charming Princess, Abricotine will soon return. She was
captured by robbers, but a young Prince saved
her."

"You are a clever little parrot," answered the
Princess with considerable surprise, "but you are
evidently mistaken and Abricotine will punish you
when she returns."

"I shall not be punished," replied Leander, still
imitating the bird's voice. "She will tell you all
about the stranger who saved her and was so eager
to enter your palace and change your notions about
the wickedness of all men."

"Really, parrot," exclaimed the Princess, "it is
a pity you are not always so entertaining. I should
love you dearly!"

The Prince smiled to himself and would have

continued the conversation had not Abricotine entered at that moment and flung herself breathless at the feet of her royal Mistress. Soon she was relating her adventures and describing her rescuer in the most favorable terms.

"I should have hated all men, dear Princess," she explained, "if I had not seen that one!"

The Princess answered never a word, but Leander could see that her thoughts continued to turn upon Abricotine's rescuer; and he felt more cheerful at this. He followed her about the palace, seating himself beside her when she paused, and walking with her in the gardens where she kept her favorite birds. On his travels the Prince had learned to imitate their notes and soon he was giving the musical calls of many rare ones such as she had never heard. This puzzled her so much that she

112

called Abricotine to her to ask her if she had brought any strange, new birds with her.

By this time Leander suddenly began to feel very hungry, and so when one of the ladies-in-waiting spread a sumptuous meal before Bluet, the Princess's pet cat, he saw a chance to satisfy his appetite. Seated at a little table with gold plate and lace napkin spread before it, the cat was served in state.

"Oho!" said Leander to himself. "So a great blue Tomcat who probably never caught a mouse in his life, and who certainly comes of no better family than I, has the honor to sup with my beautiful Princess! Is it fair that I should enjoy only the smells while he munches the tidbits?"

With that he quietly lifted the cat to his lap, seating himself in the armchair. Nobody observed this, for he still wore the little red hat. The Princess piled her pet's plate with partridge, quail, pheasant, and every delicacy, and each time she did so the food disappeared in a twinkling. All the court marveled, and agreed that there had never been a cat with such an appetite. Sometimes Leander would hold a fork concealed in the cat's paw and so help himself to larger quantities, and Bluet would mew plaintively. Then the Princess would call her attendants to heap still more upon the plates.

"See how he cries for it!" she would exclaim,

while Leander laughed in his sleeve at the success of his adventure.

Later he had the satisfaction of hearing the Princess call Abricotine to her and privately question her more fully concerning the stranger who had saved her from the robbers. Now Abricotine was a shrewd girl, who saw the turn her mistress's thoughts were taking, and she described the young man in even more glowing terms than before. The Princess was impressed in spite of herself, though she still insisted that nothing could induce her to break the peace of her palace by allowing any man to set foot in it. Little idea had she that even at that moment the handsome Prince stood close beside, listening to her every word!

During her account of her wanderings, Abricotine had described some monkeys she had seen playing among the branches of trees in the distant forest, and since the beautiful Princess had expressed curiosity to see them, Leander spent the night wishing himself there and hunting the little creatures. With considerable difficulty he captured a dozen of various colors and put them into a great sack. After that he wished himself in Paris, where he had a little coach fashioned of gold with flame-colored harnesses for the monkeys who were to draw it. He also visited a famous puppet master and bought of him two more marvelously trained monkeys, one to act as driver and one to sit on the velvet cushions.

PRINCE SPRITE

The rest, he dressed as pages. Such a sight was never seen before.

By this time it was morning, so he wished himself back on the Island. Soon the little gold coach and the monkeys came rolling into the Princess's bedchamber. Her delight knew no bounds, but she grew more and more mystified, especially when the little monkey coachman handed her a note, which proved to be a poem to her own charms. Now the two trained monkeys did a little dance together,

and so droll were their antics that the Princess laughed till she was ready to swoon. Satisfied with his night's work, Leander found a quiet room where he lay down to sleep, though only to continue his dreams of the fair mistress of the palace.

115

Upon waking he noticed a fresh piece of canvas and some colors near by. Immediately he set to work painting a picture which should surprise the Princess when next she entered the apartment. Accordingly he pictured himself upon one knee, holding a small miniature upon which he painted her portrait in the most exquisite manner. His eyes were fixed on this admiringly, while in his left hand he bore a scroll with the inscription:

"Her image is more perfect in my heart."

The Princess — Printaniere
as drawn by — Prince Sprite

PRINCE SPRITE

Imagine the astonishment of the Princess when she entered the room and beheld for the first time a picture of a young man! And then to recognize her own portrait and read the inscription! She did not know what to make of such a strange occurrence, and her first thought was that Abricotine must have done this. But when Abricotine was called in, though she at once pronounced it an excellent likeness of her rescuer, she protested that she had no idea how it had come to be in the palace.

"Some demon must have brought it here," said the Princess, trembling a little.

At this Abricotine, wishing to discover the true state of her heart, suggested that they burn the picture immediately.

"That would be a pity," answered the Princess, "when it adorns my apartments so charmingly."

But Leander, who had been the unseen witness to this little scene, decided to remove his painting from possible harm and hid it away at the first opportunity in another part of the palace.

The days that followed passed for him in a sort of trance of enchantment. He was scarcely ever out of the presence of the beautiful Princess, and he continued to take his meals from the cat, Bluet, which puzzled the entire court by the amount of food it could apparently consume without growing fat. Indeed, the poor creature seemed to be slightly thinner of late, a fact which worried its indulgent

119

mistress. Her mind, however, still turned upon the mysterious stranger, whom she now admitted to herself she longed to see. But Leander knew that the moment for showing himself to her had not yet arrived. Night after night he journeyed over the whole world, wishing himself now in China, now in Egypt, now here, now there, wherever he could bring back the richest treasures to beautify her palace. Money was as nothing to him; his rose supplied all he could dream of needing. With each new marvel that he brought, the Princess grew more mystified until at last she confided to Abricotine that she did not know what had come over her palace.

"It is most certainly bewitched," said she. "My birds talk rationally. I have only to form a wish to have it instantly granted, and I have been presented with the portrait of your rescuer. What does it mean? And who can possibly take such pains to do all this for me?" Then, with a deep sigh she added, "I can only think that this invisible being must be some monster, since he dare not show himself to me."

So the days passed swiftly. Meanwhile ugly Furibon, on his part, was busy with schemes of his own. He was still in love with the Princess although he had seen only her portrait. Only one of the four wicked messengers he had sent to spy on the Palace of Peaceful Pleasures found his way back, and he gave such a dismal account of all that had happened that most men would have turned their backs forever on such a place. But the King had just died, and Furibon was his own master now, and more obstinate and headstrong than ever. So he raised a vast army and set himself up as general to ride at their head. A ridiculous general he looked, too, in all his hideous deformity and elaborate trappings, more like one of the monkeys that Leander had brought back for the Princess's amusement than a recently crowned King.

When tidings of the approaching army of invaders reached the Princess in her palace she lost not a moment in sending her faithful Abricotine to summon aid from the Kingdom of the Fairies, where her mother lived. But she was very angry upon receiving the message from her daughter asking for aid and advice. She cried out that all her care had been in vain.

"Do not imagine that I am not aware of the change that has taken place in my daughter's affections!" she cried. "She is loved by the Prince Leander and loves him in return. I have no power over those who love mortals, so I can do nothing to save her now."

Abricotine returned to the Princess with these bad tidings, and the whole palace was in a state of confusion and despair. Leander, still keeping himself invisible, looked pityingly at the Princess's distress. He dared not speak to her at such a moment, but remembering that one of Furibon's worst faults was greed, he set out to meet him with a large sum of money. He wished himself back in the forest where he had left his horse, first assuming the dress and appearance of one of the palace attendants. As soon as he called out: "Graylocks! Graylocks!" he heard a joyful neighing and the horse came prancing and leaping to meet the master he had awaited so long. But so perfect was the Prince's disguise that even the horse did not recognize him at first. Naturally it was easy to deceive others and upon his arrival at Furibon's camp, word was sent to him that a young lady who had come from the Palace of Peaceful Pleasures demanded audience of him. So Furibon hurried into his royal robes and sat himself upon his throne, where he looked for all the world like a large toad pretending to be a King.

Leander began his address by saying that the Princess preferred a life of peace and quiet to one of warfare and would willingly pay him any sum he might name, provided he would go away without molesting her. On the other hand, if he refused this offer, she would certainly defend herself against him.

Furibon replied that he was willing to take pity on her and would protect her. In return she need only send him a hundred thousand thousand thou-

122

sand millions of pistoles and he would return to his own country.

Leander replied to this, with a careless shrug, that it would take far too long a time to count a hundred thousand thousand thousand millions of pistoles, but that he had only to say how many rooms full he would like, as the Princess was too rich and generous to be bothered with counting and weighing gold.

Furibon was dazed by such magnificence, but he decided that he would take all he could lay his hands on, then kill the messenger and continue his advance on the Princess's palace. Accordingly he said he would like thirty large rooms to be filled to the ceiling with gold pieces before he could retire with his army. Thirty rooms in the palace where he had taken up his residence while on the campaign, were cleared and made ready. Then Leander, retiring, shook his rose again and again and again till the very air was filled with showers of falling gold, while Furibon watched in ecstasy the thirty rooms filling with their golden store. When the last one would hold no more he gave a signal to his guards.

"Arrest her! Seize her!" he cried. "She has brought me bad money!"

But as the guards rushed forward with swords upraised—quick as a wink, the little red hat was on, and Leander disappeared. Bewildered, the guards ran out into the surrounding woods to search for their victim, leaving Furibon alone. Leander immediately seized him by the hair and cut off his head at a single blow. Still holding it in one hand he wished himself back at the Princess's palace again.

Now the Princess was walking in her gardens, thinking sadly of the message her mother had sent her and of the terrible fate that probably awaited them all, when she suddenly saw a human head poised in mid-air with nothing apparently supporting it. This astonished her even more than any of the other strange things that had taken place and what was her greater amazement to see the head laid at her feet by unseen hands. At the same time she heard a voice say to her reassuringly:

"Fear no more, charming Princess. Furibon will never harm you."

Abricotine, who was standing near by, recognized Leander's voice and cried out eagerly that this invisible being and the stranger who rescued her were one. At this, the Princess showed great delight and surprise.

"If it is true that they are one and the same," said she, "nothing will give me greater joy than to prove my gratitude."

"And I shall labor still more to be worthy of it," he answered.

With that, he returned to Furibon's army. The moment he appeared among them in his own form,

124

all the officers and soldiers came crowding about to welcome him with shouts of joy. Nothing would satisfy them till they had crowned him their King; then, after he had distributed the thirty rooms filled with gold among them, and ordered them to return to their own dominions, he hastened back to the Palace of Peaceful Pleasures.

It was late and Leander was weary with the day's adventures, so he laid himself down to rest, forgetting for the first time to put on the invisible hat. The Princess awoke early and descending to the apartment alone came upon him lying there asleep. She had no difficulty in recognizing him as the handsome young man in the portrait which she had studied for so many days, but she found him in reality far better to look upon. She was just about to awaken him, her hand was even outstretched to do so, when her fairy mother burst into the room. Her anger was so great at the sight before her eyes that she seized her daughter and would have borne her away to Fairyland forever had not the fairy Gentille appeared at the same moment. Her powers of magic had told her of the Prince's need and she had hastened to his side.

"My dear sister," she said, embracing the fairy mother, "I am sure you have not forgotten the good service I did you when after marrying a mortal you could not return to your Kingdom, and I made it possible. Pardon your lovely daughter now and

125

consent to her marriage with this young King, who saved me from a cruel death. Their days together will be as a tissue of gold and silk."

"Dear Gentille," cried the other, "I will consent to anything you wish."

With these words she embraced her daughter and Leander. The fairy Gentille was in a transport of joy, and all her attendants and the ladies-in-waiting of the palace came hurrying to join her in songs of triumph. It was agreed that the Palace of Peaceful Pleasures and all its marvels should be transported to Leander's new kingdom, and the two fairies promised to visit them frequently and to shower still greater gifts and blessings upon them.

But no one in the whole palace was happier than Abricotine, who had never for a moment doubted the future happiness of her beloved mistress and the Prince; and in this she turned out to be perfectly right.

THE
GOOD LITTLE MOUSE

THE
GOOD LITTLE MOUSE

ONCE upon a time there were a King and a Queen who loved each other so much that they had never been known to disagree on a single subject. Whether they hunted or fished or banqueted, whether they danced the bourrée and paven or attended the opera, their hearts were always in perfect unison. And seeing such harmony, their subjects followed the royal example, one and all. It was the happiest of times. No wonder the kingdom was called "The Land of Joy" and its fame spread far and wide.

But it happened that those in the adjoining

129

kingdom lived very differently. It was known as "The Land of Tears" and the King of it was a sworn enemy to even the most innocent pleasures. He had a grim countenance, a wild and flowing beard, hollow eyes, and a stern mouth. His body was all skin and bones and he always dressed in black, which made him look even more terrifying as he went abroad to torture and condemn his unfortunate subjects. His only joy in life was to inflict pain and unhappiness; and when he could think of no new cruelties to add to the discomfort of his own people, he fell to thinking of his neighbors in the happy land bordering his own miserable country, and he determined to make war upon it. So he called his generals and his armies together and, after ordering enormous cannon to be cast, prepared for his campaign.

The news of his approach threw the Happy Kingdom into a state of consternation, but the good King reassured his weeping wife, and buckling on his sword, set off with all courage to meet his enemy. Alas, he was no match for his cruel neighbor, though he fought with skill and spirit. One day the Queen, watching anxiously from her battlements, saw a courier riding posthaste toward the palace.

"The King is dead," he cried to her, "the battle is lost; the wicked King is marching upon you!"

At these terrible tidings the Queen swooned.

THE GOOD LITTLE MOUSE

Her grief was so pitiable it would have softened any heart but that of her stern conqueror, who marched not only into the palace, but straight into her royal chamber. Here he seized her rudely, throwing her over his shoulder as if she had been a sack of corn. He carried her down the marble steps and set her behind him upon his fierce jet-black horse. When she begged him to have mercy upon her he only mocked her helpless state. So he bore her off into his own country.

He would have had her hung before all the people, but word reached his ears that a wise fairy had prophesied that his prisoner would have a most beautiful daughter, the fairest in the whole world, and the King determined that his own young son should have nothing but the best when it came time for him to marry. So the poor, disconsolate Queen was shut up in an ill furnished room at the top of a high tower. Here she was forced to spin from early morning till late at night without a single soul for company and only three boiled peas and a bit of dry bread to keep soul and body together. She grew pale and wan with mourning over her fate till at last one evening as she bent over her spinning wheel, she saw a sleek little gray mouse creep out of a hole in the floor. In her loneliness she was glad to speak to the tiny creature.

"Alas, poor mouse," said she with kindly politeness, "what have you come seeking here? My jailer has given me only three boiled peas to eat to-day and they are scarcely enough to keep me alive. This is no place for you unless you would fast."

But the little mouse paid no heed to this and only began to dance and caper in a more gay and lively manner than she had ever seen. Indeed the Queen was so amused by its antics that she forgot her own misery for the time being.

"Here, Little Darling," she said, holding out her last pea to it, "eat this. It is all I have left for my supper, but I give it to you willingly."

The little mouse accepted this morsel graciously, but no sooner was it gone than the Queen saw upon the table before her a plump, crisply roasted partridge and two jars of sweetmeats.

"Truly," exclaimed the Queen in astonishment, "one small act of kindness is handsomely rewarded!"

She ate the delicious food, being careful not to forget to throw some of the tidbits to the mouse, who after nibbling them, grew more lively than before supper. Next morning it was still scampering about the Queen's room when her jailer brought her the three peas which he had arranged in a large dish to tantalize her. After he had left the little mouse ate up all three, also the bit of dry bread, so that when the Queen began to grow hungry for her dinner there was not so much as a single crumb. She could not help feeling a little annoyed with the mouse.

132

But as she lifted her hand to place the cover on the empty dish, she saw it fill before her very eyes with all manner of good things. These she ate with relish till she fell to thinking once more of the cruel King into whose power she had fallen, and this thought as usual completely took away her appetite.

A day or two later as she leaned from her high window, she was addressed by a queer old woman who stood beneath, wrapped in a long, dark cloak. She promised to aid her in escaping from the hands of her captors. All that this strange old woman asked in return was the gift of one sleek, fat mouse to eat, for she confessed to a great fondness for mice. The Queen was astonished at this and indeed sorely tempted to part with her gray visitor. But she could not bring herself to hand it over to such a fate.

"There is a little mouse that comes to visit me each day," she said, "but it is too good and pretty a creature to kill. No, I cannot make up my mind to harm it!"

"Very well, madam," answered the old woman crossly, "then you are not to be pitied. Keep your mouse for company. I shall have plenty without yours."

And she went away storming and muttering.

When the little Princess was born she was even more beautiful than had been prophesied. Not only this but her disposition was so happy that she laughed when most children cry. The poor Queen almost forgot her own misery at sight of her child's beauty and gayety. With the help of the good little mouse she had fashioned a small basket of woven straw. In this she placed the child, after first writing on a bit of paper pinned to her dress: "The name of this unfortunate infant is Joliette."

As she was shutting the basket lid, what was the Queen's surprise to see the mouse jump in beside the child. She was even more surprised, when she began to scold it, to hear it answer her in a human voice:

"Do not regret your kindness in keeping me from the jaws of the old woman," it said. "I may not be as unworthy of your friendship, dear madam, as you imagine."

As the Queen looked down at the tiny creature she saw its little muzzle begin to take the form of a human face before her very eyes, while its paws became delicate hands and feet. All at once she recognized it as a kind fairy who had once before tried to aid her.

"I wished to try your heart," explained the fairy, "and I have discovered it to be good. You are worthy of my friendship, for we fairies seek human companionship only when it makes life more sweet."

"Can it be," cried the Queen, "that one so rich

134

and powerful should ever lack for human friendship?"

"Many love us only for their own gain," answered the other, "and that means little to us. But when you loved me as a little mouse it was from no thought of reward. I wished to prove you still more, so I took the form of that old woman. Yes, it was I who spoke to you from the foot of the tower, and you were faithful to me."

With these words she embraced the Queen and kissed the little sleeping Princess.

"My child," said she, "I endow you with gifts that shall make you the joy and consolation of your mother. You shall be richer than your father ever dreamed and live for a hundred years—always

135

beautiful, without sickness, without wrinkles, and without ever becoming an old woman."

Enchanted at this, the Queen thanked the fairy, begging her to take Joliette away with her to keep as if she were her own daughter. This charge the fairy gladly accepted, and she lowered the child from the tower window in the straw basket. Now she must assume her mouse's form in order to climb down the rope after it. But when she had done so and reached the ground what was her con-

sternation to find not a sign of the basket and its royal contents.

"Alas, all is lost!" she cried to the Queen. "My sworn enemy Concaline has carried off the Princess. She is a cruel fairy who hates me and, since she is more powerful than I, I know not by what means I shall be able to recover Joliette from her clutches."

When the Queen heard this saddest news of all she was ready to die of grief. But in the midst of her tears the jailer and wicked King appeared. The latter, seeing that she had outwitted him and that the child had been spirited away, stamped his foot and declared that she should be put to death in-

137

stantly. He had her bound and dragged into the nearest wood, where he himself climbed a tall tree in order to fasten the rope for her hanging. But the kind fairy, who had followed under a guise of invisibility, gave him a push when he had reached the topmost bough. Down he fell in a great rage, knocking out four of his teeth. While his courtiers were hunting for them to put them back again, the fairy carried the Queen away with her in a flying chariot.

They flew till they came to a beautiful castle where, if she had had Joliette by her side, the good Queen would have been able to forget all her trials. So time passed, and though they tried by every means, they could not find where Concaline had placed the Princess. Fifteen years and more were gone now and it was reported that the wicked King's son had fallen in love and set his heart upon marrying a humble keeper of turkeys, though the girl herself was said to object to the match. However, the wedding dresses were being made and it was to be the most splendid marriage that had ever taken place in the kingdom.

Now it was so surprising that a poor turkey girl should refuse to become a Queen that the fairy decided to see for herself how matters really were; and since she wished to take the girl unaware, she once more assumed the form of the little gray mouse. Into the poultry yard she went and found

138

the girl, dressed in coarsest linen, with bare feet and an old kerchief round her head. All about her on the ground were spread dresses of cloth-of-gold and silver, with diamonds, pearls, ribbons, and laces. Her turkeys were trampling and pecking at them all the time the wicked King's ugly son was standing above her, saying roughly: "If you refuse me your heart, I will kill you."

And to this she answered him proudly:

"I will not marry you. You are ugly and more cruel than your wicked father. Leave me in peace with my turkeys. I love them better than all your fine clothes."

The little mouse looked at her with admiration, for she was as beautiful as the sun. As soon as the King's son had gone the fairy took the form of an old shepherdess and approached the girl.

"Good morning, my dear," said she. "Your turkeys look like very fine ones."

The young turkey girl smiled at the old woman very pleasantly and answered: "They want me to leave my turkeys for a paltry crown. What would you advise me to do?"

"A crown is very beautiful, my child," said the fairy, "and you know neither the value nor the weight of it."

"Ah, but perhaps I do know," replied the girl, "and that is why I refuse it though I have no friends or relations in the world."

"You are good and beautiful, my dear," said the wise fairy, "and that is worth ten kingdoms. But tell me, I beg you, since you have neither father nor mother, nor friends nor relations, who placed you here."

So the girl told her how it had all come about: how for many years she had been kept a prisoner at the mercy of the cruel fairy Concaline, who beat and abused her unmercifully, so that at last in desperation she ran away, preferring any hardship, even death itself to the unhappiness of her lot; how as she sat crying in a wood the King's son chanced to pass that way and took her away to tend the

140

turkeys in the royal poultry yard; and how without any wish on her own part he had come to love her so much that her life had become almost as much of a trial to her as it had been before. And the fairy listened to this story, hardly able to believe her ears.

"But tell me," she asked, "by what name you are called."

"I call myself Joliette," answered the girl, "at your service, madam." And she dropped a pretty curtsy.

At this the fairy could have no further doubts, so throwing her arms about the turkey girl's neck she kissed her affectionately, saying: "Joliette, I knew you once long ago. I am delighted to find you so gentle and intelligent, but I wish you were cleaner, for you look like a little scullion! Take these beautiful clothes lying here and put them on at once!"

Joliette obediently threw off the old handkerchief from her head and shook down her fair hair, which was as golden as sunlight and as fine as silk and which fell in ringlets to her feet. Then, dipping some water from the fountain in the poultry yard in her two delicate hands, she washed her face till it became clear as an oriental pearl. Straight as a rush she stood, with the color of roses in her cheeks and lips.

When she had put on a fine dress, the fairy

could scarcely believe that her own eyes could be beholding such a miracle of beauty.

"Have you any idea who you are, my dear Joliette, now that you are so fittingly dressed?" she asked her.

"Truly," replied the girl falteringly, "it seems to me that I must be the daughter of some great King."

"And would that make you glad?" persisted the fairy.

"Yes," replied the girl with another curtsy, "I should be very glad."

"Well," said the fairy, "rest content. More than this I may not tell you till to-morrow."

So back she flew to the castle to bring the good news to the Queen, who was busy with her silk-spinning.

"Will your Majesty give me that distaff and spindle for my own if I do not bring you the best news you have ever had in all your days," she cried out.

"Alas!" sighed the Queen. "Since the death of the good King and the loss of my daughter Joliette, I would not give a pin for all the news in the world."

"There is no need for you to grieve any longer," the fairy told her, "for all is well with the Princess. Only just now I have seen and talked with her, and she is so beautiful that she has only to say whether or not she will be a Queen."

144

Then she related everything she had heard and seen from beginning to end, and the Queen cried with joy to know that her daughter was so beautiful, and with grief that she should be tending turkeys in a barnyard.

"When we ruled in our happy kingdom," she cried, "the King and I never dreamed that our child should spend her days as a poor turkey girl."

"That is all the doing of the wicked Concaline," the fairy told her. "It is to spite me that she has put her there; but she shall not stay in the poultry yard after to-morrow or I will burn all my books of magic!"

"And I will never agree to her marrying the son of this cruel King!" vowed the Queen.

Meantime the King's son, being very angry with Joliette, sat down under a tree near the royal palace and howled with rage and grief at his failure to win her. His father heard him and went to the window to inquire the cause.

"What makes you sit there crying like a great fool?" he demanded.

And the Prince answered, "Our turkey girl will not love me."

"How now! She refuses to love you!" cried the King. "I will make her love you or she will die!"

So he called his guards and gave them strict orders.

"Fetch the girl here and I will make her suffer so she will repent her obstinacy."

They marched to the poultry yard, and there they found Joliette in a white satin dress embroidered in gold and diamonds and more than a thousand yards of ribbon. Never had they seen such a fine lady, and the sight of her tied their tongues so that they dared not address her.

"Tell me whom you seek here," she asked them politely.

"Madam," said they, bowing low, "we are looking for a miserable little wretch called Joliette."

"Alas, it is I!" said she. "What do you want of me?"

At that they seized her and bound her with thick cords hand and foot lest she escape before they could bring her to the King. Even he could not but be a little moved at sight of her beauty; still he was too cruel to have much mercy on any one. So he began taunting and heaping abuse upon her, insisting that unless she would agree to love his son she should be publicly beaten. On her knees she begged for mercy, asking that the King give her two or three days to consider what she ought to do. The King and his son agreed, at last, to shut her up in a high tower; but it was at this moment the good fairy and the Queen arrived in the flying chariot. When they heard all the news the Queen began to weep again, saying bitterly that misfortune was always following her and that she would rather see her child dead than married to this cruel son of a wicked father. But the fairy whispered in her ear:

"Take courage. I shall worry them into a state of frenzy and you shall be avenged."

She was as good as her word. That night the wicked King had no sooner settled himself in bed than the fairy transformed herself into the little mouse again, hiding herself under one of the pillows. The moment he fell asleep she began to worry and annoy him. She bit and scratched and drove him into a state of fury. While he cursed and raved, his courtiers hunted in vain for any sign of a mouse. The ugly son fared no better, till at last he leaped from his bed and taking his sword rushed into his father's apartment, crying out murder and brandishing the weapon this way and that. The gentlemen-in-waiting fled in terror and the King and his son fell upon one another, half crazed and blinded as they were. So in the end they wounded one another and fell to the floor, bleeding. At sight of this all their subjects who had long hated and feared them, and who had only obeyed their wishes through terror, bound them with stout rope and flung them both into the river to drown. Thus died the wicked King and his son.

The fairy, having done her work well, now changed her mouse's form for her own and hastened to the black tower where Joliette was shut up

under more than forty locks and keys. But the fairy
had only to strike the great outer doors three times
with a little wand of hazel wood. Instantly that and
all the rest flew open. Behind the last one of all they
found the Princess, still very sad and forlorn. The
Queen flung herself upon her neck, crying:
"Joliette, my dear daughter, I am your mother and
the Queen Joyeuse." And Joliette listened to all
that had befallen them at the hands of the wicked
King with wonder. She could scarcely believe so
much good news after all she had suffered, and she
fell at the Queen's feet, showering her with tears
and a thousand kisses. Then she affectionately em-

braced the fairy, who had brought her baskets full of jewels, gold, diamonds, bracelets, pearls, and the portrait of King Joyeux set in precious gems.

"But let us lose no time," urged the fairy. "Let us go into the state hall of the Castle and show ourselves to all the people."

She herself led the way in a dress with a train more than ten yards long. The good Queen walked next all in blue velvet and gold, with a still longer train, for they had brought their robes of state with them, and the Princess Joliette followed last, a marvel of youthful beauty and modesty. So they proceeded to the palace, curtsying graciously to all they met. Crowds followed them, marveling and wondering who these three fine ladies might be.

When the hall of state was full to overflowing the good fairy rose and told the people that she would give them King Joyeux's only daughter for their Queen, the beautiful girl they saw standing before them. Further she promised that they would be happy under her government, and that, should they accept her, she would herself find her a husband worthy to be their King, one who should always be cheerful and banish melancholy from every heart. At this the cheers rang long and loud and the words on every side were the same: "Yes, yes, she shall be our Queen. We have been sad and miserable too long!"

Such was their reception and never had there

been such happiness and rejoicing in the kingdom before. Next morning, when the Princess woke in the palace, there was the good fairy ready to present her to the handsomest Prince that had ever been seen; she had gone to the very end of the world in her flying chariot to fetch him. And the minute the Prince and Joliette set eyes upon one another they loved instantly and with all their hearts. So "The Land of Joy" and "The Land of Tears" became one happy kingdom at last and the wedding was celebrated amid the greatest rejoicing.